Case Histories

A Portico Paperback

Case Histories

STORIES BY
ALEXANDER KLUGE

Translated by Leila Vennewitz

HOLMES & MEIER
New York / London

Published in the United States of America 1988 by
Holmes & Meier Publishers, Inc.
First paperback edition 1991

Holmes & Meier Publishers, Inc.
30 Irving Place
New York, NY 10003

Great Britain:
IBS
International Book Services Ltd.
Perth Street West
Hull HU5 3UA

Originally published under the title *Lebensläufe,* copyright © 1962 by
Henry Goverts Verlag GMBH, Stuttgart, Germany. "Korti," the final
selection in *Lebensläufe,* does not appear in this edition. Selections
appearing in this edition that did not appear in *Lebensläufe* are:
"Attendance List for a Funeral," "Sergeant Major Hans Peickert"
(published as "Haupt Feldwebel Hans Peickert" in *Akzente,* vol. 2,
Munich: 1963), and "Mandorf" (originally published as "Mandorf" in
Merkur, no. 187, September 1963). First English edition published
under the title *Attendance List for a Funeral* by McGraw-Hill Book
Company (1966).

This book has been printed on acid-free paper.

Library of Congress Cataloging-in-Publication Data

Kluge, Alexander, 1932–
  Case histories.

  Translation of: Lebensläufe.
  I. Title.
  PT2671.84L3613   1988   833!914   88-16259
  ISBN 0-8419-1045-6 (acid-free paper)

Manufactured in the United States of America

translator's acknowledgement

I wish to express my very grateful thanks
to my husband, William Vennewitz,
for his help in translating this book.

Leila Vennewitz

Vancouver, Canada

Contents

foreword

The stories in this volume question tradition
from a number of very different aspects. They
are case histories, some invented, some not
invented; together they present a sad chronicle.

Alexander Kluge

Additional translating assistance
was provided by Mr. Michael Roloff.

Introduction

Radically experimental, Alexander Kluge's writings, films, and other creative activities have contributed greatly to the development of contemporary Central European intellectual life. Although recognition of his achievements has been slow in coming, he is now recognized as one of the leading lights of the German cultural scene. Indeed, on November 22, 1985, Kluge was awarded the Heinrich von Kleist literary prize in Berlin—a prize whose past recipients include Bertolt Brecht, Robert Musil, and Anna Seghers.

Born in 1932, Kluge was the only son of Ernst Kluge, a physician, and his wife, Alice, who settled in Halberstadt, now part of the German Democratic Republic. The war years in Nazi Germany were traumatic for the young Kluge and left vivid, if not disturbing memories. Situated in Kluge's home town in the Hartz mountains were divisions of the "Junkers" airplane armament industry and the Buchenwald concentration camp, designed to provide slave labor for that industry. Toward the end of the second World War, in early April 1945, a massive Allied attack left Kluge profoundly shaken: less than a dozen yards away from him a bomb exploded, and more than three-fourths of Halberstadt, including his parents' home, was leveled. Kluge was to return to this shattering experience time and again in his fiction.

After the end of the war, his parents divorced and his mother entered a second marriage to a lawyer living in Berlin. Therefore Kluge accompanied his mother to Berlin, where he attended high school in the city's western sector. In 1949 he enrolled at the University of Marburg, choosing law as his major, history and church music as his minors. Later Kluge transferred to the Goethe University in Frankfurt am Main, where he became a student of Theodor W. Adorno, co-founder and a prominent exponent of the Frankfurt School of "Critical Theory."

In addition to Adorno, Kluge was influenced by Walter Benjamin and Bertolt Brecht at this time. It was from Benjamin and Brecht that Kluge profited most in shaping his film theory. In general, all three German exiles, who had fought against fascism, stimulated his questioning of the German past and how it still played a role in the German present. Not only did Adorno impart to Kluge his advanced critical thoughts on the culture industry, but he also provided a connection to another exile, Fritz Lang, who helped Kluge during his internship at the Berlin CCC Film Studio.

Kluge's many-faceted career and creative personality emerged in the 1960s. Since that period, cinema and various cultural activities have been as important to Kluge as his literary ones, and they form the basic context for his writings. He teamed up with Peter Schamoni of the noted German filmmaking family, for his first short, *Brutalität in Stein* (Brutality in Stone, 1960). While ostensibly a documentary about the monumental architectural efforts of the Nazis, this short attempted, through montages and structural ironies, to reexamine Nazi ideology. The following year the film won a first prize at the International Short Film Festival in Oberhausen. In 1962, together with a circle of young German filmmakers at the same Oberhausen forum, Kluge initiated a reform manifesto that led directly to the movement known as the Young German Film, which culminated in the new German Cinema of the 1970s and early 1980s.

Reversing the artistic decline of German film in the immediate postwar years by raising its quality and cultural prestige was the initial intention by the Oberhausen group, and Kluge still plays a central role in pursuing this objective. As a filmmaker he has a dozen feature films and numerous shorts to his credit. Most of Kluge's films demonstrate the possibilities of an original and quasi-literary cinema. Their sound tracks seem to exist as an essential, independent channel rather than as undercurrents that are subordinate to the visual. The films yield unique features without conventional plots, roughly suggestive of Resnais's *Hiroshima mon amour,* and they are characterized by montages that create playful breaks and, at the same time, superimpose an important level of consciousness and memory. The films defy facile interpretation after a single viewing; they are recherché films or vehicles of cinematic research whose single most distinctive personal style is a thorough blending of documentary and fictional elements.

In addition to working in film production, Kluge has distinguished himself in the field of cultural analysis by writing more than five book-length studies over the last decade and a half. Some of these relate directly to his creative projects. For instance, *Öffentlichkeit und Erfahrung* (Public Sphere and Experience, 1972), jointly authored with philosopher Oskar Negt, shares, with the 1973 film *Gelegenheitsarbeit einer Sklavin* (Part-time work of a Domestic Slave), a concern with institutional pressures that prevent women from maintaining traditional modes of production in the home. Kluge returned to the theme of the oppression of women in his 1300-page book of social theory, *Geschichte und Eigensinn* (History and Obstinacy, 1982), also co-authored with Negt. For more than twenty-five years, then, Kluge's work has constituted an artistic and intellectual primer of the West German cultural scene. To appreciate Kluge's unceasing drive, one needs to keep in mind that he has also continued to practice law, not infrequently allying himself with protest and grass-roots causes. And in the early 1980s, a man in his early fifties, he married for the first time and now has two children with his wife, Dagmar Steurer.

In many respects Kluge exemplifies the new "publication pluralism" *(Veröffentlichungspluralismus)* that transcends individual media in general and West German films and literature in particular. In the close union of media, primary and secondary versions can hardly be divided; they exploit double or even multiple renderings of the same material. For instance, Kluge based his first feature film *Yesterday Girl* (1965), on "Anita G.," a story from his first published work, *Lebensläufe* (Case Histories). He drew his feature *Strong Man Ferdinand* (1976), a satire on excesses in industrial security at a high point of terrorism in the Federal Republic during the 1970s, from his short narrative "Big Business Bolshevik" from his prose collection *Lernprozesse mit tödlichem Ausgang* (Learning Processes with a Fatal Outcome, 1973). And *Die Patriotin*, which focuses on a Hessian high-school history teacher's forays into Germany's past, appeared in print and on the screen in the same year (1979). Novelization of film and cinematic techniques in fiction begin at this point to lose clear distinctions. Kluge's reworking of text materials in various media resembles the production methods used by American media corporations. Both suggest a new horizon in simultaneous realization and release by different media.

Considering the close interrelation of Kluge's literary and cinematic production, it will come as no surprise that his major themes and fundamental techniques are incorporated in these two artistic forms. Common themes include: tensions between the individual and institutions (legal, commercial, political, and military); the individual's struggle for stability and fulfillment in the face of conflicting instincts, needs, and pressures—imposed by bureaucracies, regimes, and economic systems—beyond his or her understanding or access; the individual's vain endeavor to orient himself or herself either in a private labyrinth of impulses, desires, and self-deceptions or in the collective bogus order and reality in the grip of an ideology; the German people's moving forward into a threatening future against a background of both a divided Germany and a national past deformed by National Socialism. In short, Kluge explores the tensions and pressures of modern industrial society as much as he creates from a consciousness burdened by the Nazi past.

Kluge's fundamental approaches to prose and film exclude naive storytelling and action-packed plots. His narrative structure is unique, offering a dry, jolting, and disjunctive account. For instance, in *Case Histories*, "The Princess," "Discussion with the Fest Coordinators," and "Twelve O'Clock" serve as headline introductions to three successive sections of "Manfred Schmidt," in which the title character presides over a carnival party. According to Kluge's poetics, such *Stationenprosa* corresponds to the functioning of human consciousness—a staccato, skipping, disjointed, noncontinuous perception, a perforated presence. Both Brecht's "mini-unit" composition and the influential theoretical writings of German experimental novelist Arno Schmidt furnished the model for this anti-discursive writing style.

The montage principle, Brechtian distance, and Arno Schmidtian literary mosaic characterize the key formal aspects of Kluge's prose. These formal qualities lend themselves to the condensation typical of short stories, Kluge's prose fiction domain. Short prose in general favors the pregnant moment—much like the mini-unit structure made familiar by Brecht. *Case Histories* exhibits most of the major themes and fundamental techniques of Kluge's short stories and has been revised since its first publication in 1962, when it contained nine "histories." In 1974 Kluge produced a new edition containing nine additional stories, including "Case Histories." Thus the present English edition, with its eleven stories, does not fully correspond to either of the German editions but is closer to the original collection, expanded by three stories: "Case Histories," "Sergeant Major Hans Peickert," and "Mandorf," which Kluge first published in literary journals after 1962. (Kluge's continuous text revisions resemble Brecht's analogous text recastings.)

Almost all the texts in this collection cover the period from the Third Reich to the Federal Republic. The title story, "Case Histories," deals with protagonists profoundly affected, traumatized, sometimes even killed by the Third Reich and the Second World War. Their lives or their memories reveal continuities with present-day West Germany. Sergeant Major Hans Peickert, the protagonist of this story is executed during the final phase of World War II for black marketeering. But in 1962 a veterans' gazette resurrects him as the military hero who had procured the diesel fuel to insure a roll-back of the front by a Panzer division, commanded by a famous general, which had been immobilized by lack of fuel. "May this issue of the Bulletin display the spirit that Hans Pieckert, holder of the Knight's Cross, has bequeathed to us as a priceless legacy!" Society, Kluge suggests, fails to draw the logical conclusions, namely, that the military spirit lives on, even if its individual representative has been destroyed.

The stories in *Case Histories* show a restorative post–World War II West German society. Not all the protagonists represent conservative, reactionary, or pro-fascist leanings, but three besides Peickert do. In "Demise of an Attitude," Chief of Detectives Scheliha, who hotly pursues a criminal in the throes of the Third Reich's collapse, and, in "Lieutenant Boulanger," a failed medical student turned officer, who sought out, selected, and

executed Red Army commissars of Jewish descent for the purpose of Nazi "race research," illustrate society's failure to learn
from the past. Neither Scheliha nor Boulanger are punished for
their deplorable acts during the Nazi regime.

In all of his fiction—just as in his films, which in this respect
differ radically from the internationalism of Herzog, Wenders,
and the present-day Schloendorff—Kluge's focus is national. He
tells the story of Germany, a national mosaic composed of individual case histories. His political critique of the German restoration after 1945 was not unheard of in the West German literature
of the early 1960s that had Günter Grass's *The Tin Drum* and
Herrich Böll's *The Clown* offering devastating critiques of West
Germany's economic miracle as well. But it was Kluge's unusual
technique that assured him of critical attention. Any reader who
samples the Posa text can easily attest to the anti-discursive,
"unpasteurized," impure narrative style. Five short case histories
(Dr. von Posa, von Hacke, Baronin von Posa-W., von Kirchheim,
Fräulein von Posa), a historical chronicle (the Posa family), and a
police report (Gerda von Posa-E.) assume the terse authenticity
of documentary material. (Elsewhere in the collection, Kluge
goes even further in this nonliterary direction, quoting in "An
Experiment in Love" at length from a volume of Nazi documents
about medical experiments on people.) It is true that Kluge
alternates this nonfiction and quasi-public sphere of discourse
with views of the heroine's inner world, but the reader senses that
the story transcends conventional literary tone, genres, and form.
Kluge frequently couches the inhuman acts of 1933–1945 in
legalese, a parodistic device that often implies an ironic protest
against the "documents."

"Fräulein von Posa" and the remainder of the collection
transgress traditional literary forms of communication by employ-
ing cinemorphic modes of perception and editing that lend a
novel appeal to Kluge's prose. Within deceptively objective passages, shifts of perspective take the reader from historical chroni-

cle to sudden close-up. Reading about the surviving younger generations of Posas we are made to see "the same mouth, shadows around the mouth, the same inquisitive eyes, dark golden-brown, prematurely graying hair, temples throbbing when excited, veins at the temples." The close viewing range and nuances of light and color correspond to film language just as the cinematic shorthand does. In addition to these techniques related to detail, the larger units of Kluge's stories also employ cinematic principles by accumulating separate narrative units that, like the sequences in motion pictures, are not linked by transitions and often represent different perspectives. In short, by shifting "camera angles" and perspectives, using light effects, cuts, montage, and editing, Kluge's stories follow film form.

Attesting to the growing importance of Kluge's writing as early as 1967, Hans Mayer, who has been a prominent German literary critic and historian since the Second World War, entitled one chapter in his critical study of German literature since Thomas Mann "Speculations and *Case Histories*." In addition, other writers of such stature as Enzensberger were soon penning "Case Histories." And the respected "Bibliothek Suhrkamp" accorded *Lebensläufe* the recognition of republishing it in its Modern Classics series.

Thus Kluge has contributed to the literary Zeitgeist, but he also differs from his contemporaries in the school of documentary literature. Like Peter Weiss in the stage production of *The Investigation* (1965), Kluge attempted on the printed page to unmask the hidden Klaus Barbies and to bar the return of the Joseph Mengeles. Formally both Kluge and Weiss were considered part of the flowering of nonfiction writing across all literary genres that started in the early 1960s and lasted for over a decade in West Germany. Kluge's *Description of a Battle* (1964), his second collection of short stories, seemed to exemplify such documentary even more than *Case Histories* did. Kluge shifted his approach from case histories that examine a society to the macro-organization of an army of the past, and its impact on the individual soldier. The volume describes the historic defeat of the German Sixth Army at Stalingrad, a crucial event in the decisive turning of World War II against Hitler. Kluge arranges a variety of material: guidelines for carrying on war in winter, interviews with survivors, letters, pages from diaries, sermons by army chaplains, and medical reports, for instance, into a collage evoking the downfall of the German forces. Even though the emphasis may have shifted from *Case Histories* to *Description of a Battle*—from the individual toward the collective—the inescapable nexus between individual and institution remains the prime focus. Catastrophes in the individual case histories sprang from the inner force of the social system, from the logic of institutions, in the same way that the German defeat at Stalingrad resulted from the historical consequences inherent in the caste-oriented military mentality of Prussia and of the German officer corps respectively.

Certainly Kluge's literary creations impart a heightened sense of historical reality. But documentary is only one element— a significant and overt one—among numerous others. For example, two more elements are the examination of German tradition and the provocation of the reader to question the historical material. In *Description of a Battle* both the technique of dialogue-like questions and the montage of conflicting information lead the reader to look for information beyond the material supplied. Still another element is that like a ventriloquist, Kluge frequently employs the discourse of documents, especially those from scientific, military, administrative, legal, and economic experts. Frequently his ends are a kind of intellectual black humor. In essence, then, Kluge challenges the facade of objectivity and authenticity that characterize contemporary West German documentary literature.

In the 1970s Kluge continued his literary examination of what makes German citizens learn "to adapt themselves to disaster." The title of a new collection of stories, *Learning Processes with a Final Outcome,* points to the author's skeptical assumption that Central European society, if not modern post-industrial man as a whole—despite the individual's pursuit of happiness—is collectively programmed for catastrophe. The collection continues the portrayal of the German 1933–45 mentality. Indeed, "Sergeant Major Hans Peickert," which Kluge did not publish in the German editions of *Case Histories,* appears in slightly shortened form in *Learning Processes.* More important, some stories begin to look beyond German borders and reflect new contemporary problems and different kinds of people—for instance, the *Freizeitmensch* (man of leisure) and the constitutional or industrial security agent. Plant security expert Rieche Snuff (the literary twin of the title character of Kluge's movie *Strong Man Ferdinand*), in the employ of a multinational corporation, becomes as zealous and dangerous as the terrorists to whom he ultimately owes his job. The title story of *Learning Processes,* the last one of the collection, illustrates that humanity in general has not learned from history: after civilization has wiped itself from the face of the earth in a nuclear confrontation, the survivors continue the same struggles intergalactically.

This skeptical world view also underlies Kluge's prose collection of the 1970s, *New Stories,* which bears the subtitle, "Uncannyness of the Times." While *New Stories* does not approach science fiction to the degree that *Learning Processes* does, both collections reflect Kluge's predilection for dealing with the Third Reich and contemporary topics.

By the beginning of the 1980s, Kluge's prose fiction reflected a change from the verbal text to a mixed medium composed of text and visuals. The covers, proportions of printed images to text, and distribution mode of the books published since then were aimed to provoke readers or upset their conventional views. At this stage of Kluge's literary work a reader would be much less likely to mistake his particular blend of document and literature for sheer documentarism—his work of this decade simply does not square with conventional notions of realism. Kluge has variously defined his style as an antagonistic realism or a realism of protest. "Realism," he once stated in an essay on his method, "is not a natural condition. The natural condition is ideology, dreaming. Whenever I protest against the reality principle, i.e., against what reality is doing to me, I'm being realistic. Therefore my motive for being realistic is antirealist."

For Kluge, realism reflects conflicts and is constituted just as much by wishes, dreams, and historical utopias as it is by facts. These wishes, dreams and utopias are not only part of reality, but they enable readers to envision the possibility for creating a different social reality. His latest work, *Bestandsaufnahme: Utopie Film* (Taking Stock: Utopia Film, 1983) shows to what extent that Kluge has incorporated a Freudian dimension and subjective factor in his documentary style. Whatever the new tone and new world view may be, Kluge continues to raise disturbing questions about German social realities, and he remains one of the most significant voices of protest in the contemporary German cultural scene.

HANS-BERNHARD MOELLER

Case Histories

THE CAST

Adrienne E.

Mary Vierlinger †

Elisabeth Packer

John Vierlinger

Annabelle Glaube

Jakobine Freitag

A. Bierstadt

Schwänchen

J. Bierstadt

Otto Glaube

Katrin B.

D. Albers

F. Albers

Chr. Albers

A. Gütersloh

Gerda Fritzsche

Gerda Schwickers, née Ermolly

H. Fritzsche (a friend of books)

Marta Glaube †

Martha Bierstadt, married to
    Koch (Eastern Germany)

A. Fritzsche

Ernstchen Ermolly

F. Glaube

Lisbeth Gütersloh

M. Ermolly

P. Ermolly

Aunt Herta Ermolly

Aunt Bühne from
    Hoppenstedt

Deesdorf, journalist, with

Son and daughter

Barlepp, Lieutenant

Ernst Belve

Neidthart Belve

P. Glaube

Margaret Gueffroy,
    née Glaube

B. Haul, née Ermolly

A. Haul

Attorney

Two family doctors

Business friends

Musicians

Servants

Attendance List for a Funeral

Who is afraid?
Adrienne: not afraid
A. Bierstadt: afraid
S. Bierstadt: afraid
Katrin Bierstadt: afraid
Jakobine: afraid of devaluation
D. Albers: afraid
Annabelle Glaube: formerly afraid, now aggressive
Ernstchen Ermolly: not afraid
G. Fritzsche: not afraid
Deesdorf: afraid when he makes a mistake
F. Gütersloh: afraid

Do the relatives love anyone?
Adrienne: no one

Ermolly: no one
A. Bierstadt: no one
Jakobine: not sure
Ernstchen Ermolly: thinks he loves F.
Annabelle Glaube: no one
Katrin Bierstadt: no one
Belve: no one
D. Albers: in the line of duty, all those in need
F. Albers: possibly his wife, but probably no one
F. Gütersloh: no one

Mary Vierlinger, the deceased, never had a chance to get married, i.e., her parents kept her at home. At the most intense culmination of her flowering, Mary was abjectly in love with a certain female. This person later became very stout. Mary made another new will. She never wanted to see this person again. After her unfortunate passion for this person she remained in her unhappy state with her parents (as if love as an escape from the paternal-maternal hive was refuted by this first attempt). By the time Mary had passed her thirtieth year her parents were too old for her to leave them. She surrounded them with care; she was carefully watched over throughout the day by herself and her parents, by six eyes, that is; when she left the house she accounted for the time she spent as well as the money she spent, nor did she believe that a momentary escape from this domination would bring her happiness. At fifty she could imagine no other life than this, a life that followed the parental rhythm. After her mother died, in 1939, following her father's death a year previously, Mary Vierlinger, a true member of the Packer family, was free for the first time in her life. Her parents were duly consigned to the earth. Mary immediately bought a Chevrolet. She took a trip to Italy going as far as Bari. The sudden outbreak of World

War II once again thwarted Mary's impulses. During the war she was occupied with charitable work, as befitted her station in life. Here she followed the pattern of her sister Adrienne. In March 1943 Mary was awarded a decoration. To the very end she could not believe the English would bomb the town of the former Packer and Vierlinger factories. When they did, however, she fought stubbornly for the continued supplying of the damaged hospital to which she was attached.

For years she maintained a certain level of alcohol in her body. The dinner table, fully extended, was always set for guests who never came. There were two old armchairs which Mary had had taken up to the attic in 1936. Air-raid precautions required these objects to be taken down to the cellar in 1939. Empire furnishings for five rooms had also been saved. In 1944 Mary had her parents' bedroom furniture chopped up as an air-raid precaution. In 1950 Mary was sixty-three years old. She ate little, drank less now, refrained from buying a car. She spent most of her time caring for her heirlooms. Within a few years she developed a vein inflammation that necessitated the amputation of one leg above the knee. No one thought Mary would survive. Untapped vitality, never used, was concentrated in a diminishing space. Then, on behalf of Mary, whose life had been spared, the family, more particularly her kind sister Adrienne, made inroads on the capital of the Vierlinger fortune; she obtained a power of attorney and tried to make life easier for her sister. A special basket chair, on wheels, was designed for Mary. Mary developed an insatiable appetite. She was supposed to have plenty of visitors to distract her. Without her cravings being in the slightest degree satisfied, after six years in her basket chair Mary suffered a series of strokes. She went on trying to speak. Behind the almost closed lids lurked a now unleashed determination to stay alive. Her left, i.e., remaining leg, was amputated below the knee on account of gangrene. Mary made a good recovery from the operation. Two years after her last stroke she died.

Adrienne Ermolly was unnerved by her sister's first amputation; the subsequent strokes, her sister's increased determination to stay alive, and finally the long-drawn-out hours preceding her death, with the dying woman (who until the very end had recordings of Beethoven concertos played to her) stubbornly defending her life, put her in a panic. If she had read about such a case in a newspaper or magazine she would never have related it to herself. She would have been curious if she had been told about a death of that kind in a film, for example. Now her sister's lingering death struck at her own resources. Adrienne placed her own way of life, i.e., herself and her children, in a state of siege, that is to say, she allowed none of her own family to approach her sick sister: Adrienne herself avoided her sister. Mary was looked after by a "faithful" servant, in other words a person whom the Vierlinger family had for decades made dependent on themselves and who was no longer capable of leading her own life. If it had not been for the servant and one of the gardeners, who also caught sight of Mary Vierlinger from time to time, Adrienne would have said that Mary was already dead. Adrienne armed herself (she being the most threatened one of all) with the tried and true weapon of irritation ("you wouldn't recognize poor old Mary," "you wouldn't recognize that poor old hunk of flesh"). Oughtn't Adrienne to ask the family doctor to put this creature out of her misery? As a protection against such thoughts, Adrienne did not even consult the Vierlingers' family doctor, who might have acted on the suggestion; for Mary she consulted only the leading professors at the university hospital, men whom she could not approach with suggestions of killing. So Adrienne sealed off the rising panic in her heart, removing the traces of Mary's calamity by obliterating every last memory of Mary. She was worried lest a trace of Mary should remain in her, in Adrienne herself, possibly in the form of a psychogenic illness, or lest one day she too should become like Mary. The danger of having been the last person to watch the sick woman seemed to her so great (like the passive listening to a curse, but then there's no such thing as magic) that she spent four weeks at a sanatorium under the observation of first-class doctors. In the country air, at the Sanatorium W. situated on wooded slopes in Hesse, she observed herself for a month, analyzed the past few years. She analyzed Mary's problems to see whether they could be hers too. As had been her intention, she arrived at a negative conclusion. Regenerated by the crisp country air, tanned by long August afternoons on the terrace at W., she returned to the Ermollys, with the principal aim now: to take charge of the funeral service for Mary's cremated remains.

How had the drive to the crematorium been arranged? The relatives-by-marriage from the Thuringian branch of the family, the Glaubes, the Fritzsches, the Albers, and the Güterslohs, suggested that they be driven there ahead of time so that the cars would be available to take the Packers and the Ermollys. The guests waited in a rather small waiting room in front of the chapel; Adrienne did not even want to go into this waiting room, as it was too bare. She had her own car and the one carrying the closest relatives wait in front of the crematorium entrance until the manager and the pastor—Albers, a member of the Thuringian branch of the family—came for her when it was time. The crematorium building consisted of a squat white tower, made to look like a church, from which smoke rose. In front of this building were a colonnade and a forum. Adrienne placed her hand on Ermolly's arm as he led her across the forum and they entered the chapel itself. Those who had been ushered in here from the waiting room all rose to their feet.

The hired musicians played "Christ is risen" behind a screen. Strangers or staff members appeared in the side doors and immediately closed the doors again when they saw they were disturbing a service. When Albers had recited the Lord's Prayer, all present rose to their feet; Adrienne and her entourage placed flowers on the coffin. The musicians played "In the midst of life we are in death." The coffin sank from sight. In an anteroom adjacent to the chapel Adrienne received the condolences of the guests. The manager sent someone to ask whether any of the flowers were to go to the Ermolly home. Adrienne declined. After their condolences the guests repaired to the Hotel Prinz Eugen. A table for thirty-four guests had been prepared. The members of the family remained there from 4:30 P.M. till well into the evening. Pastor Albers was handed a sealed envelope by Adrienne containing an appropriate sum of money.

A. Bierstadt (aloud): I think Gerda wants to leave the room. *Antonia* (to herself): Just imagine, just imagine. *Adrienne* (aloud): Please don't make so much noise! Some musicians enter the dining room and start playing a solemn piece of music. *Adrienne* (to herself): When Ernstchen has a tan, his cheekbones stick out (aloud): I think we can all get up when the music's over. *A. Bierstadt* (aloud): That's very nice. *Ermolly:* Your very good health! *Pastor Albers:* The same to you! *Lisbeth Gütersloh:* The whole service was very dignified! Trouble-maker *Annabelle Glaube,* doyenne of the Thuringian branch (to herself): She is seventy-six, pale delicate features: What was in the envelope? *Ermolly:* Do be quiet for a moment, everyone. Trouble-maker *Annabelle* (to herself):

Red patches on his neck, that looks like an early death. Maybe he has prostate trouble? *A. Bierstadt*, as if by thought transference (aloud): Prostate comes but once a year, dumdidumdi-dumdida (grasps old Ermolly by the arm and passes with him and others from the dining room to the billiard room, thence to what was known as the lounge). *Annabelle*, his mother (to herself): I'll give Albers six months, Adrienne fifty years at least, Ernstchen Ermolly will live to be an old man. For the Güterslohs I predict two deaths this year, Dora Wilke may die quite suddenly. In the lounge *Ermolly* gives signs of a slight cough that has been bothering him since yesterday; as always, his nose is rather congested, he has sinus trouble (aloud): I have it cleaned out by Professor Beier, that way I can breathe again in the evening, but by noon the next day my sinus is blocked again. But so far I can't feel anything. *A. Bierstadt* (jokingly): Take a laxative! *Ernstchen Ermolly:* And what d'you do in the evening? *Gerda Fritzsche:* Go to bed, as I have to get up early. *Ernstchen Ermolly:* I could pick you up tomorrow with my car. *Fritzsche:* No. *F. Albers:* Let's show some slides in the billiard room. *F. Glaube:...* (drinks). *Ermolly:* Your very good health. *Adrienne:* Do be quiet everyone, can't you? *Albers* (to himself): The dead will rise again and the guilty tremble....

The Thuringian members go across to look at slides.

Views of the Thuringian members:

Flowers taken from a funeral bring death to the house.

Cremation is not giving back to the earth.

Things must get better, they've been bad long enough.

No sandwiches with afternoon coffee; no drinks with lunch, maybe after lunch.

You must leave something on your plate to show that, although you've enjoyed your meal, you could have managed without it. The Ermollys ate everything on their plates. The Fritzsches, Albers, and Güterslohs helped themselves liberally, left something of everything. The Ermollys and the Packers down to and including Antonia saved pieces of meat to the end. They systematically ate the less important things first, then the more important.

Two hymns are stingy. Four or five would have been more in keeping.

The meat they served was tough!

No one mentioned these things; but they poisoned the atmosphere.

Adrienne's rules of thumb

If I were desperate I would first try having a good sleep. If that didn't help I would get a tan; when the circulation gets going, things start looking up.

By the time the dinner hour came round, none of the guests at the funeral could remember Mary Vierlinger, they had occupied themselves too much with the deceased during the day. What they still saw in their mind's eye was: D. Albers giving his sermon, Adrienne sitting in the first car (wearing a large black raincape), the taxis driving up, the people streaming out, as if emerging from a government office, on their way to the Hotel Prinz Eugen.

Search for the culprit!

Actually no one was to blame for Mary's death. A. Bierstadt said: Mary ate too much meat. If she had done some gardening all that meat might not have hurt her. The Thuringians, inasmuch as they reflected at all, saw in Mary's death a punishment for the arrogant Packers. Mary's death, said Pastor Albers, was not premature. This phrase was open to numerous interpretations by the Albers, the Fritzsches, etc. Annabelle

Glaube did not care one way or the other about who or what was to blame. She did not reckon with her own death and so was not conscious of Mary's death. Antonia Bierstadt could not bear to spend the whole day with her relations. She longed to be by herself again. For a while she chatted with the servants in the hotel kitchen. F. Gütersloh blamed the pressure in his stomach, which he found very painful during the slide-viewing, on the rather tough lamb that had been served; besides, the hour of 4:30 for the evening meal was not well chosen.

Attorney W. said: Allow me to express my heartfelt sympathy, and that of my wife. The death of your dear sister, whose property I administered, was a profound shock to us all. The Packers' family physician, Dr. von Bo, joined in: We still find it hard to believe. Adrienne to the attorney: Will you let me have an accounting of my sister's property tomorrow? I would like to have these things at home. Thank you for looking after my sister's affairs. Turning to the doctor: You did what you could. The doctor suspected Adrienne of having made her sister's death easier. Perhaps, said Adrienne, it was best after all, the way it happened. Albers said: That's how we have to look at it. The attorney was offended because Adrienne had deprived him of his trusteeship.

The covering up of the mirrors in the Prinz Eugen, although no religious ceremony was performed here, was at the request of D. Albers. The lights in the rooms where the slides were shown were also somewhat dimmed. The three musicians from the municipal theater were fed in the kitchen of the Prinz Eugen. Adrienne paid them after they had declared themselves satisfied with the food and drinks they had been served.

It was a dignified funeral, said two of the Vierlinger business friends. Well thought out, said D. Albers. Just as the deceased would have wished it, said one of Mary's old friends who had turned up although Adrienne had not invited him. Altogether a most dignified end, said the former mayor of H. It occurred to Adrienne that actually Mary had not wanted any religious service. But it would have been difficult to dispense entirely with the ceremony. Without a ceremony the parting from Mary would have been less final. Although Adrienne could not see that she had any choice in the matter, she was afraid now of the real or supposed feelings of the deceased.

Grieving for lost possessions in Eastern Germany

A property in Erfurt, which had suffered bomb damage but was very extensive, registered owner Fritzsche. Two properties, parcels with road access in Quedlinburg, which Annabelle Glaube had earmarked exclusively for her boy Otto. A glove factory in Ha, not entirely the property of the Güterslohs, together with a villa, unfortunately expropriated. Mortgages held by the Fritzsches on houses in Wegeleben and Wernigerode. Garden, rectory, abandoned to the Reds, in Quedlinburg, belonging to D. Albers.

Christine Albers never forgot that summer's day when she lost her husband. She still could not believe that the thin-lipped man with the slight beard would never wake up again as he had always done in the past. She was already hurrying to put on some coffee when she told herself: now I can be sure he is dead. He had to be buried quickly because of the summer heat. That same evening (of the day he died) men came to take him away. As long as he was in the house Christine felt she could not raise her voice. She did not want to show any joy either, rearrange the old pictures or move the furniture that his tyrannical will had held immovable for sixteen years. She was afraid of being punished. For instance, she did not want her husband to emerge from a closet and catch her in her altered feelings, after hiding her real feelings from him for sixteen arduous years. Next morning she had a long leisurely breakfast. A few days later she gave a dinner for the funeral guests at a restaurant, since she did not want them to come to the house and see how such and such an armchair was not placed alongside such and such an article of furniture, etc. The following day she found out that for the time being she could not get at house or bank account. Her husband had appointed someone else as executor. Thus her way of life was restricted even after the tyrant's death that had at first seemed to promise so much.

Did the family have anything else to brag about?

A supervisor, a furniture dealer, two nephews in uniform, various nieces, a teacher, and a journalist with a son and daughter.

What did Adrienne's guests not get done?

D. Albers: Completion of a chapter of his evangelical apologia. Chr. Albers: A visit to the doctor, a visit to the executor, collecting a small sum of money. A. Gütersloh: Teak contracts with the firm of S., G. & K. in Rei; an inspection of the timber yard. A. Bierstadt: Visits to the sick, coffee at old Mrs. Th.'s, sandwiches at old Mrs. Steinrück's, giving a heart injection. Antonia: Lying down, piling sleep on sleep, till the mouth gets moist on its own, then a cup of coffee! Joler Bierstadt: Mild giddiness desired, by means of hot mustard, beers, inhaling ether, violent swinging, studying or any other kind of work, movements that become harder and harder to follow, driving from the country into a new town: this kind of giddiness confuses one's view of the limited possibilities at one's disposal. Jakobine: She could burst into tears at the thought of all the things she does wrong. How she mismanages food, success, convalescence, friendships, looking back over the past sixty years. And then she would die, rather earlier than necessary because of a wrong way of life. Jakobine had no desire to see films depicting the lives of several generations, for the thought of the ephemeral nature of existence wiped out all her enjoyment. Two Fritzsches and two Bierstadts were sitting with Ermolly in the kitchen among the servants. They were brought back from these more relaxed surroundings. Fritzsche: Plunge into a book. Better still: Enter a dark room, a movie. The hope here: to emerge different from the way one entered. If he read, he would be conspicuous among the funeral guests.

See you soon, said Annabelle to Adrienne as she left; Adrienne said nothing, she knew that Annabelle, the doyenne of the other side, camouflaged her hostility by an apparent senility. Most of the relatives pecked each other on the cheek as they took their leave.

Anita G.

Don't you know a more cheerful story?

1

The girl Anita G., crouching under the staircase, saw the boots when her grandparents were taken away. After the capitulation her parents returned from Theresienstadt, something no one would have believed possible, and founded factories in the vicinity of Leipzig. The girl attended school, looked forward to a normal life. Suddenly she became frightened and fled to the Western zones. Of course she committed thefts. The judge, who was seriously concerned about her, gave her four months. She only had to serve two, the rest she spent on probation in the care of a probation officer. This woman was overzealous in her duties—the girl fled to Wiesbaden. From Wiesbaden, where she found peace and quiet, to Karlsruhe, where she was pursued, to Fulda, where she was pursued, to Kassel, where she was not pursued, to Frankfurt. She was apprehended and (there being a warrant out for breach of probation) transferred to Hanover. She escaped to Mainz.

Why does she constantly infringe on private property as she travels? She appears under a variety of names in various police departments' all points bulletins. Why doesn't this intelligent person regulate her affairs in a satisfactory manner? She moves from one rooming house to another, mostly she has no room at all because she quarrels with the landladies. One can't drift around the country like a gypsy. Why doesn't she behave sensibly? Why doesn't she stay with the man who is making a play for her? Why doesn't she face facts? Doesn't she want to?

2

She took the man she had met the previous day up to the room which was no longer hers. Here, this way, she whispered, hearing him grope cautiously behind her in the dark. He could not move without making some sound. He was not very adept anyway. She moved toward him in this darkness and, taking him by the hand, led him past her former landlady's quarters to her own room. She locked the door and switched on the light.

The man disapproved of all this fuss, but he did not know the reason for it. He probably thought she was anxious not to disturb the relatives she was staying with. He would have preferred to call on these relatives and regularize his new contact with this attractive girl. He was not one for secrets. In fact he told her so. But she didn't want to explain to him just now why this room was no longer hers. Frau Schepp's reasons for evicting her, or why the girl had given up the room of her own accord and thereupon been evicted by Frau Schepp, couldn't be explained in a few words. Frau Schepp: large, unusual hat, large eyes full of little vanities and a hard sparkle. Her husband, at least that's what some people say, flung himself off the third-floor balcony while she was busy in the next room. Maybe Frau Schepp counted on the girl sneaking back in? The girl moved about the room without making a sound, which for her was easier than being noisy; she was one of those people who lack the imagination to make a noise. The man bumped into the iron bedstead. She trembled at the thought of Frau Schepp.

The warmth and security emitted by the body lying beside her did not reassure A. The pale, coarse skin, the close-set nipples, surrounded by separate, long fine hairs, seemed themselves in need of protection. She had no protection to give. If it did not concern her personally in some important aspects, she might even find this man ridiculous—his anxieties, his fear of embarking on something illicit. She lacked the ability to take her time selecting the people she really wanted to be with. Impatiently she accepted anyone prepared to take an interest in her. It was a chance to restore her life to a state of security and order. That was why she wanted to preserve her advantage.

She felt chilly in the unheated room, and the prospect of the cold she would come down with was enjoyable and at the same time unwelcome, because it would be a nuisance, something like having a baby—she sought the warmth in the body lying beside her which she had to get used to all over again. She was not shy with him now. She let him have any part of her body he wanted. She gave herself with a simplicity that even simple people do not possess, and took care that what she told about her past sounded natural. She arranged her past in such a way that it could not upset him. She made no plans, she merely waited for his suggestions for the next day. Touching the thin quilt she reassured herself that the body was still sleeping beside her. While he was there she slept outside the quilt, at the edge of the bed, lying on her side and leaning lightly against the pile under the quilt; she was afraid that otherwise she might disturb him with her movements, which she could not control during the night.

Toward morning the man woke up and turned to her again. She would have liked to spare him this exertion because under no circumstances did she want him to do more than he wanted to do himself. She did not want this night, which might be the last, to leave a bad taste in his memory. But on the other hand she could not very well deny him if she wished to be simple and natural. She made an effort to appear interested, but was not very successful. She was so anxious to know what he would say that she missed what he said to her. She pulled the quilt up over the exhausted man and reproached herself for not having been of use to him. She nestled up to the quilt and waited till he had fallen asleep. Whatever happened she did not want to take advantage of him. Most of all she did not want to take advantage of him in this particular way, which was of no benefit to her.

She could move without making a sound, and also open each lock without a sound. The man stumbled as she let him out, but this merged with the morning noises of the house. It broke her heart to watch him dress in the chilly room, but there was nothing she could do about it since she was not even supposed to use the room. She let him go quickly, so that these moments would not be etched in his memory. As soon as he had gone, she also left this apartment.

3

She wanted to see him once more before she left town. For many weeks she had been prolonging this relationship from day to day, although her situation in the city was becoming increasingly dangerous. She went to look for him and after a time found him in the café opposite the Cathedral. He still looked tired, slack mouth and hollow, drawn-in, "frosted" lips. A rather trite conversation. To a man sitting next to him: He had been on night shift..., when you go to bed with a passionate woman.... He was not aware of her nearness.

She was taken aback. So this was all that love accomplished. She wished she had left the day before. No matter how much of her strength she invested in this man, he remained a blank. She despaired of his ever being useful to her. She accompanied the man at a distance to the government offices into which, as was his daily habit, he disappeared. Later on she calmed down. She decided to give it one more try.

4

The background can be sketched in briefly.

She would never have exchanged one word with this man if the accident had not brought them together. On the day in question in May 1956, A. wanted to leave Mainz because she had got into debt at a number of rooming houses near the railway station, and for various other reasons no longer felt safe in the city. Before leaving the city she visited the university, which was situated on a rise. She passed the day sitting in the university lounges and attending lectures. She wanted to go to Wiesbaden and possibly get a job there, but at the university gates, as she was crossing the street, she was struck by a car (she may also have walked into the car). She picked herself up and examined the abrasions. The car owner walked up to her and slapped her face. She did not know how to react. Later on she got to know this man better. Had it not been for the accident she would never have talked to him at all. The man encouraged her to remain in Mainz and look for a job and a place to live. He was anxious she should have enough money and a job. He was afraid that otherwise her inactivity might prove an obligation. Although he categorically rejected any kind of obligation, he failed, during the subsequent course of this relationship, to exercise the proper caution. She noted the consequences of his carelessness but kept this fact to herself, probably because she was afraid of his reaction; besides, he did not ask about it.

5 Looking for an attorney

The girl's attention had been drawn to a newspaper article describing the career of the Frankfurt attorney Mr. Sch. She went to Frankfurt and tried to get in touch with this defense counsel. However, he could not be reached at his office all morning. In the afternoon she saw him from a distance at the courthouse, the attorney's head clerk having advised her to look for him there. She did not dare speak to him when, surrounded by a covey of questioners, he left the courtroom and descended the wide staircase. Later that afternoon he was still not available whenever she phoned his office. She did not want to make an appointment for one of the following days, she had already given up hope of being able to see the famous man and interesting him in her case. She refused to talk to one of his junior associates because she had confidence only in the counselor himself, and besides she believed that only he could dispense advice free of charge. Her mistake was that, at the very beginning—the first time she phoned, in fact—she had been too diffident. That explained why the office staff had given her the brush-off.

The counselor's day

The famous man spent the morning wandering about his apartment in his dressing gown. He was not curious about the new day. He telephoned Wiesbaden and Zürich and then sat down at his desk.

His hand lay on the desk, resting on the second and fifth fingers, thumb quietly at the side, third and fourth fingers kneeling. As he slowly raised his fourth finger and brought it forward, there came a moment when the two kneeling fingers snapped forward together and the hand fell flat on the desk. He did not answer, waited until the secretary gave up knocking and went away from the door. Thick veins on the back of his hand, which was narrow with a few hairs on it; the two kneeling fingers thrust forward, and the hand lying flat, out of breath, so to speak, on the desk. He looked at it, he was not curious about the day.

Later on some associates needed his approval of an urgent decision. He took part by telephone in a discussion concerning a remission of sentence at the Department of Justice. The telephone calls stimulated him a little. If he feigned interest in these discussions long enough, he became interested. One after another his associates phoned him and asked his advice. He was not in the mood. A forceful person cannot be enlightened. How weak must a person be to be enlightened?

The middle part of the day ran according to a schedule which he was able to influence only by postponing his departure from one meeting or appointment to the next; his chauffeur, however, who maneuvered him expertly through the afternoon traffic, partially recouped this lost time. His two co-counsel were waiting for him at the entrance to the courthouse. He followed them to those terrible courtrooms. The exhausting performance at lunchtime, now over, had tired him. This performance was exhausting because, as well as wit, intelligence, astuteness—qualities which, incidentally, he did not really possess—he was obliged to display fortitude in drinking and eating; the very opposite of his talent for maneuvering. Part of his popularity was based on these pretended qualities. He approached the accused on the stand with ambivalent emotions, spoke to various people before reaching his seat, then turned around to greet the accused in the usual manner. The two co-counsel turned the pages of the briefs. He withdrew to the furthest corner of the bench to see whether there was a draft there. The accused was questioned. He was a fat, well-paying businessman who was brought up on a morals charge. The defense counsel stood in front of his table waiting to see if he should intervene. His movements were as stealthy as if he had to catch or measure something. He was tired, he stumbled over his words when he spoke, turning half toward the accused and half toward the judge's bench, and all the while, with subdued catlike tread, as if not to frighten away an idea of insult or hurt or alarm anybody, he paced up and down on the polished floor in front of the counsel table. He found it hard to concentrate. The judge and jury became restless. The judge did not like him. It was his name that kept them in line. He stumbled over his words several times, and the whole performance was really not very prepossessing, during his pleadings the judge leafed through his papers. How could he harm him?

When judgment had been handed down, attorneys and others surrounded him like a swarm of admirers and shielded him from awkward questions. The accused thanked him. In the hallway a number of people approached who wished to speak to the counselor. He hunched his shoulders because he was afraid of the drafts in the hallway, nevertheless he stopped to chat to some of those who addressed him. That afternoon he was supposed to drive out with the District Attorney to the State Mental Hospital, as he thought he had discovered a case there which necessitated the intervention of either himself or the District Attorney. Instead he sat for a time with the District Attorney over tea.

This tall, well-protected man, who did not have many more years to live, made little use of his influence. He had more influence than he would admit to himself. About this hour of the evening he began to perk up a little, in the late afternoon he had taken drops which stimulate the heart for conversation and widen the arteries. In no respect could he be said to be a specialist, not even in his capacity as an attorney, because nowhere was he prepared to feel secure; but he had specialized insofar as all his power was concentrated on combating the pogrom that might be unleashed again at any time. This power could therefore be drawn on solely for the purpose of warding off danger. He had another five years or so to live and for this length of time did not need to exert himself unduly. He knew enough ways of getting by. He could stay aloft, so to speak, motor idling, until he glided to the final landing, if this is a fitting comparison. That evening he went to bed early. He could still have wielded a great deal of influence, but there was nothing he wanted. He wanted to return to the womb. He did not believe in change; in fact, as long as he was not in danger he was against change, as one never knew whether it might not be accompanied by danger.

Need for protection

Very thin limbs under the impeccable suit, very hairy because he had needed this protection during the first minutes of his life; no one had thought at the time that he would live; his trousers are suspended from his spine and, without touching his body at any point, hang down to his slightly splayed feet.

Covering up, pretense

Sits in stockinged feet, although nobody knows this, well hidden by his desk, and lets his eyes light up, "signals" when his visitor makes a remark, he has not been listening and is pretending; it is necessary for him to impress this visitor, but not essential. The visitor is one of those people with whom, although they have no power over him, he does not on any account wish to be at odds.

Hostile Nature

He hunches his shoulders, not because it is cold but because no one knows what to say to warm him up; he looks round for a draft, a justification for his craving for warmth. He is afraid of catching cold. He cannot afford any weakening to his physique. He is shielded from people but vulnerable to drafts.

Cowardice

For over an hour the discussion, over which he was presiding, had been going completely adrift because he refused to interrupt the speakers when they got off the point. Finally they were arguing at random in the order in which they rose to speak. Many were furious at the way the debate was being conducted. The best of them were annoyed at this procedure and accused the chairman of not listening. As a matter of fact he was not listening, but no one could prove this. He put up with the hostility of the good ones and refused to interrupt the speakers, what harm could the malcontents do him? On the other hand he was afraid of reprisals on the part of those he interrupted, if he did interrupt the speakers, and anyway that sort of thing was foreign to his nature. (Whenever his associates made suggestions, he usually said yes, although he could equally well have said no right away because he could equally well say no the next day, no harm could have come to him on that score, and anyway as far as his safety was concerned it made no difference whether he said yes or no; but there was also the fact that he did not like saying no, and preferred saying yes first, because there was always a chance that with time the matter would straighten itself out and perhaps he would never have to say no at all. He paid his associates to make suggestions and therefore also paid for the right to turn the suggestions down. But he would not have liked to turn down one of their suggestions, no doubt because he was afraid of reprisals.)

Stimulation

Three-hour luncheon in a restaurant near the station, where he receives guests whom he has to impress: he flatters the new arrivals by advancing to welcome them at the door and, on the way from the entrance to the tables, making derogatory remarks about the guests already seated. After lunch he talks about his death, not to everyone. The guests who heard him were not sure how they should respond. The depiction of his imminent death was his most powerful stimulant, and—just as with penicillin, aspirin, etc.—he used it without compunction.

Persecution, protégé, two alternatives

He has developed a magnificent apparatus capable of protecting him in the event of pogroms and, of course, even more so in times of peace. But how is he to keep the sensitive apparatus going if there is no persecution? He therefore needs a powerful stimulant to keep himself going. Naturally the most powerful stimulant would be a protégé who is really in danger. But how is the protégé to penetrate the protective circle of fame, associates, colleagues, office staff, this complicated organization, and get through to the great defense attorney himself?

6 The girl spends the night with her lover in somebody else's car

As he had no means of knowing where to look for her when she had no room and no fixed points at which she could be found at definite times, she waited in the street in front of his apartment until he came home in the evening. She let him go into the house, not wanting to impose on him in case he had something important to do, and when he emerged onto the street again she followed him at a distance until she was sure he was only going to the theater. She spoke to him. He was surprised and asked her what had happened. She made up some story or other. They gave the theater ticket to someone waiting outside the theater. She was so glad to have found him again that she admitted having no place to go. She mentioned some money she was expecting, in order to dispel his misgivings. She found an unlocked car and dispelled his misgivings about going for a short drive and then bringing it back to the same spot. He was afraid of being discovered and fined, but she counted on it being their last evening together and so dispelled the objections he intended to raise. This was a very grave mistake on her part, for he did not feel at ease again for the rest of the evening.

He had thought it all out and planned a thorough discussion with her that day about a more permanent arrangement. He could not find the tone of voice with which these words had originally sounded in his head, but even the disconnected possibilities at which he prodded and poked sent her into sheer panic. She wanted to put him off. This was the very thing she had been so painstakingly working toward the last few weeks; now the dream was joined by a flood of objections, an antipathy toward any idea of a more permanent arrangement. Her confused emotions swept across a spectrum of reactions, she did not know how to respond. She longed for a disaster from which she could extricate him. Or for some power to intervene and put an end to her flight, so that she could confess everything—not even confess: just gain time. She compared herself to a sorceress who draws a circle around the person she loves and carries the contents of the whole world into this circle. Her face was contorted. This frightened her, for love is supposed to smooth everything out. For an instant she doubted her love and detected signs of his deceiving and trying to get rid of her by the clever use of words.

It was his custom to separate everything he did with her into an official and an unofficial part, and he tried to undress her when he had finished his dissertation. She was not prepared for this, and behaved as if she did not know what he had in mind, since she did not want to forfeit the last evening in this way. She clung to the conversation they had been having and explained why she would like to be his wife. She said "Come here" to keep him at arm's length and talked a lot of carefully controlled nonsense. He found this very agreeable: whether she talked about their future life together or tried to please him or turned his hands away—it merely confirmed him in the direction he had taken. She tried to fend him off, but had to remain simple and natural.

For a moment she speculated on what would happen if she told him everything: the child and the police, but she could not face it. She felt it would be unfair and told him nothing about either. She released herself from his embrace in the cramped carseats and crawled out of the car. It was pouring with rain. She let the water splash onto her skin. She walked up and down. She stayed outside in the downpour until he called to her from the car. She was wet, and spoiled the up-holstery when she crawled in beside him again. This confused him. He wavered between the feelings of a car owner and the feeling of her wetness.

7

She made one final attempt to unravel her situation by asking her parents to come to Bad Nauheim from Leipzig. But in the two days which she spent with her parents she did not manage to pry them apart. They were a closed phalanx of fear of ordeals. What she needed was separate discussions with her mother and her father, but all she could get was plenary sessions. They stuck together like wet feathers, although they had never been able to stand each other and usually took every opportunity to keep apart. They were scared of being alone with their daughter for a single moment and had reached a prior understanding.

Things had gone wrong from the very start. She had wanted to freshen up in a small café and before she was ready she was discovered there by her parents, who stifled every gesture with the noise they made greeting her. She did not want to hear them make this noise, she found this as repulsive as the way they ate or noticed certain things and did not notice certain things. She tried to break through their united front. This was a failure, as the conversation was soon running on the familiar track: she criticized her parents, which did her no good. She told them they hated each other, and this only made them draw closer together, as they were afraid of hatred. The parents pointed out how harmoniously they could live together, after so many years, if the daughter would refrain from criticizing. A. wished for a disaster to sweep away the barrier which was hardening with every word. While she was still wishing this, she lost all hope of her parents ever being able to help her now. She had not realized how weak they were when they functioned jointly, how very much they had weakened each other in their marriage.

The evening of the second day in Bad Nauheim the police, who had checked the hotel register, came and arrested her. Her parents were told of the arrest by the hotel management. The following morning A. succeeded in escaping from the police station. She hurried back to the hotel, but her parents had left. They were frightened of being dragged into the affair, regardless of what it was all about. They had not left a letter, presumably because they could not agree on what to say. A. avoided the station and the autobahn since she assumed that police were on the lookout there, and she stopped a car on the federal highway to Frankfurt.

In Mainz on a street near the station she ran straight into Frau Schepp. She was hurrying along, her eyes seeing nothing, till she was almost on top of her; horrified, she stepped aside to cross the street, hoping she had not been noticed. She ran in front of a car which had to jam on its brakes, forcing other vehicles to swerve; a noise that had the same effect as if searchlights were being focused on her. She dashed along a street, on and on till she stood in front of her lover's apartment. She waited.

They drove to Wiesbaden. She was against this expedition as she begrudged them the little time she had left. After the trail she had left in Bad Nauheim it could only be a matter of days before the police got wind of her. She tried to make the best of this evening, but when they had been sitting for a short while at the "Valhalla" exchanging news (which filled her with impatience—the whores' faces, the great revolving chandelier—), the police arrived for a check of identity cards. She tried to persuade the washroom attendant to show her an exit. While she could see that some prostitutes were somehow or other managing to slip away, she was kept there with half-promises. The attendant probably took her for a serious offender who could bring nothing but trouble if one did as she asked. The girl locked herself in a toilet. She gave the attendant all the money she had on her. The police ordered everyone inside the toilets to push their identity cards under the door. They started at the left. A few moments passed, then came a "Thank you" and the scraping of feet. A. came out when ordered to and let herself be conducted to the washroom exit, where she tore herself loose from the police. She spent the night in the open, halfway between Wiesbaden and Mainz. She was afraid the bridges over the Rhine would be watched at night. By late afternoon she was waiting outside in front of her lover's apartment, to explain why she had run away. He gave her a little less than a hundred marks and advised her to head for the Ruhr area. He did not know what he ought to do. He did not want to desert her. She found this unbearable and broke off.

8

She took refuge in an empty villa, the people may have fled. Even the faucets had been dismantled, perhaps everything was to be torn down. She settled into the attic rooms and could have got away if they had come on her unawares. The anxiety and fatigue of the evening when she had found this shelter during her long walk through the city streets developed during the night into a pressure in her chest, pain even when she breathed, and heavy feverish limbs, later her whole head was affected with the grippe that has something of death about it, her eyes cold, no warmth in them, painful eyes in deep sockets, limbs prostrate, fidgety, unresponsive. She lay here with her illness almost like a dog in the empty house. She went out only once and bought some food, not because she was hungry but because she wanted to do something to sustain life.

9

From two o'clock on, the lights were turned off in this corner of the large restaurant because the noon-hour stream of customers was over. When she looked up and took away her hands from her eyes, which she had been covering to warm them, she was sitting in the dark, as if in an underground passage, but there were great beams above her and along the walls, holding up the room. She assumed it was raining outside,

sound of cars: things were happening. While she had kept her eyes shut, almost asleep, her blood had stayed sucking at her stomach walls, now it flowed back. Everything was functioning now, head, limbs. After a while she left the restaurant by a side exit which could be reached from the washroom and which, unlike the main entrance, was not watched by the waiters. A car drove up to the very edge of the crosswalk. She immediately assumed a defensive pose, her hands outstretched toward the car, which did then stop in time, as close to the edge of the crosswalk as it was allowed to come.

In the late fall A. arrived in Garmisch, where she wanted to choose the hospital in which to have her child. She reached Garmisch in one day, but that was all she could manage. The man who had driven her there and would have looked after all her expenses wanted to take her out that evening. Her nose started to bleed, and she felt nauseated. She managed to reach the washroom, where she was safe for the time being, but later on she found it impossible to be nice to the man. She did not want him.

10 Flight movements

In Bonn she worked as secretary and cashier for a studio theater. A policeman's voice over the phone asked to be put through to the theater manager. The girl thought the call referred to her. She put the call through to the manager. She took two hundred marks from the till and went North. She was still trembling in the train. In the first-class waiting room at Lüneburg, the only way she could get rid of a man who kept pestering her for a date because, due to a misunderstanding, he thought she was available, was to hand over her identity card to him for safekeeping. After this she did not dare go back into the first-class waiting room; instead she spent the night sitting up in the second-class one. The railway police tolerated her since she could produce a valid ticket; although it is difficult to speak of tolerance when they beat up and threw out a man only slightly shabbier who did not drink up his beer when ordered to do so. The railway was fully entitled to do this. A. took the first train passing through. On her flight she turned to Ulm, Augsburg, Düsseldorf, Siegen, at each of which she made only a brief stop, leaving behind small debts which spurred on the wave of persecution behind her, so that —if one looks at it out of context—she seemed to be deliberately provoking this wave of persecution in order to motivate her flight movements.

11   Flight movements

In November she worked in Brunswick until, returning to her landlady's with the five-o'clock rush, she saw police outside the house. She fled to Stuttgart.

From Stuttgart, leaving hotel bills behind, she fled to Mannheim, Koblenz, Wuppertal, avoiding Düsseldorf, from Wuppertal to Cologne, the proximity of Koblenz scared her off and she made a detour to Darmstadt.

For purposes of illicit gain she rented a room in Darmstadt, as she had done in various other cities, pretending a willingness to pay which, strictly speaking, she did not have.

12   Stripped

By February she urgently needed a more permanent place for her confinement. She tried once more in the Rhineland but, since her condition was obvious to all, no one would accept her. She gave herself up to the police, after establishing that she had no papers and could positively not manage by herself. She was remanded to the prison at Dietz. There she had to paint tiny figurines, but otherwise settled down in her protected cell. When the time came for the birth she was transferred to the prison hospital, two separate rooms. She had no confidence in the doctor because of his fibrous skin and bad breath; he was exactly like the type of hairdresser to which she did not go. She was frightened and applied to be taken back to her cell; she had found a fellow prisoner who could help her in an emergency. But the birth began before the warden's office had sent a reply. She had to let this man manipulate between her legs, but there was no time. Everything went very quickly. After two days the child was taken away and placed in an institution near Kassel. The milk was pumped off from her breasts. For a few days, still in bed, she helped sort out the evidence against her which was scattered throughout many towns. The nervous breakdown came as a surprise to everyone. She was transferred from the prison hospital to the women's ward of the university hospital, where she was treated mainly with penicillin and after a time the breakdown was brought under control.

An Experiment
in Love

In 1943 the cheapest method of carrying out mass sterilization in the camps appeared to be the use of X-rays. There were some doubts as to whether or not the infertility thus achieved was of a lasting nature. We brought a male and female prisoner together for an experiment. The room provided for the purpose was larger than most of the other cells, and rugs from camp headquarters covered the floor. Hopes that in their nuptially furnished cell the prisoners would comply with the requirements of the experiment were not fulfilled.

Were they aware that they had been sterilized?

Presumably they were not. The two prisoners sat down in opposite corners of the comfortably carpeted room. It could not be ascertained through the port hole, especially designed to provide outside surveillance, whether they had spoken to one another since being brought together. In any case they did not converse. This passiveness was particularly undesirable because some high-ranking visitors had expressed their intention of watching the experiment; in order to expedite matters the camp medical officer in charge of the experiment gave orders that the prisoners' clothing be removed.

Were the subjects embarrassed?

The subjects could not be said to appear embarrassed. Generally speaking they remained, even without clothes, in the same positions as before, they seemed to be asleep. Let's wake them up a bit, said the doctor in charge. Phonograph records were brought. It could be observed that the prisoners reacted to the music at first. Soon, however, they lapsed once more into their apathetic state. It was important that the subjects get started since this was the only way of ascertaining whether the unobtrusively induced infertility remained effective for prolonged periods. The staff members associated with the experiment waited in the passage a few yards away from the cell door. On the whole they were quiet. They had been instructed to communicate only in whispers. There was always one observer at the port hole. The prisoners were to be lulled into believing they were now alone.

Nonetheless the cell remained devoid of erotic tension. Those in charge almost believed that a smaller room would have been more suitable. The experimentees had been carefully selected. According to the files, the subjects could not fail to experience considerable reciprocal erotic interest.

How did they know this?

J., daughter of a senior civil servant in Brunswick, Jewish, born 1915, i.e., 28 years of age, married to an Aryan, matriculated, studied history of art, was regarded in the small town of

G., in Lower Saxony, as the constant companion of the male subject, one P., born 1900, occupation: none. On account of P., J. left the husband who could have protected her although she was a Jewess. She followed her lover to Prague, thence to Paris. In 1938 it became possible to arrest P. on Reich territory. A few days later J. turned up on Reich territory in search of P., and was likewise arrested. In prison and later in camp, the couple made several attempts to meet. Hence our disappointment: now at last they were free to do it, and now they did not want to.

Were the subjects unco-operative?

Basically they were obedient. I would say, therefore: co-operative.

Were the prisoners well fed?

For some time before the start of the experiment the subjects had been fed an especially nutritious diet. Now they had been lying for two whole days in the same room without making any discernible attempt to approach each other. We gave them the whites of fresh eggs to drink, the prisoners drank the albumen eagerly. Group Leader Wilhelm had them sprayed with garden hoses, after which, shivering with cold, they were conducted back to their comfortable room, but even the desire for warmth failed to bring them together.

Were they afraid of the moral laxity to which they felt themselves exposed? Did they think this was a test of their moral rectitude? Did the fatality of the camp stand between them?

Did they know that, in the event of impregnation, both bodies would be dissected and examined?

It is unlikely that the subjects knew or even suspected

this. They had received repeated assurances of their survival from the camp authorities. It is my belief that they did not want to do it. To the disappointment of Group Commander A. Zerbst and his staff, who had come here for this purpose only, the experiment was a failure, since all measures, including force, produced no positive results. We pressed their bodies together, held them so their skin barely touched while the temperature was gradually raised, rubbed them down with alcohol, fed the subjects alcohol, red wine with egg, even meat, also champagne; we adjusted the lighting, yet none of this brought on erotic excitement.

Did we really try everything?

I can vouchsafe that we tried absolutely everything. We had a group leader among us who knew something about such matters. He tried one thing after another, measures never known to fail. We could not, after all, go in there ourselves and try our luck, since that would have been a racial crime. None of our measures succeeded in producing erotic excitement.

Were we aroused ourselves?

More than the couple in the room, certainly; at least, that's what it looked like. But then that would have been against regulations. I do not believe, therefore, that we were aroused. We were agitated, perhaps, because the experiment was not working out.

If I love thee and surrender,
Com'st thou to me in the night?

There was absolutely no way of inducing a positive reaction in the subjects, and the experiment was therefore abandoned as inconclusive. It was later resumed with other subjects.

What happened to the subjects?
The recalcitrant subjects were shot.

Would this indicate that, at a certain level of misfortune, love can no longer be generated?

E. Schincke

I

In the years immediately following 1933, Eberhard Schincke, forty-eight years old, allowed himself to be duped by Hitler. He had read "The Threat to German Ideals," but he believed the National Socialist movement contained a core of idealism which the author of that book failed to perceive. Schincke was prejudiced against the aristocracy of the intellect. He was the principal of the Cathedral School in the small town of S. The younger members of his staff, Reh, Mortchen, and Neumann, stood politically to the Right of the National Socialists. The other teachers voted for the State Party. Schincke felt instinctively attracted by the National Socialists more so than by the positions his colleagues took. He thought, as Nietzsche has taught us to do, not only with his head but with all his senses, just as one uses more than one sense to grasp the meaning of a word, or as a woman becomes something more than an abstract quantity to the one who embraces her. Needless to say, Schincke's highly developed powers of perception were particularly bothered by the marching columns in the streets, but these were the expression, not the essence, of the movement. On the other hand, with his corpulent, elephantine build, his slouching, stoop-shouldered way of sitting, he was bound to make an unfavorable impression on the Brownshirts, although as it happened this deviation from the norm was part of the Germanic heritage, for, according to one of the most ancient Germanic sayings, the truly strong man is lethargic. A dangerous situation developed one evening when some Brownshirts lay in wait for him; but apparently this was due to a misunderstanding which was cleared up the following day. Schincke had vague expectations of this movement, the birth of a new Romanticism which, instead of being confined to a small cultural élite, would share its wealth with the masses. He realized that these masses were perhaps not suited to develop quality on their own, but an outdoor performance of *Die Meistersinger* toward the end of 1933 in front of the Cathedral, attended by a large number of the inhabitants who roasted wieners in the intermission, reconciled him and made him tingle with optimism, as opera was now climbing down into the world, so to speak, and real life was acquiring the same significance as life on the stage. It was in this state of mind that he got married in 1934. He saw, of course, that the provinces remained provincial, although on a bigger scale. He was hopeful, and at the same time concerned, that the early upheaval might actually consolidate the narrowness of life there, but it was not his way to complain about something which did not cause him any immediate inconvenience. It would have required a very powerful incentive to get him and his heavy body to oppose his entire environment, which provided him after all with his livelihood—and which the Third Reich embraced with the totality of a Hegelian concept. As with the great democracies of modern times, or some of the great scholars of the nineteenth century, it was as difficult to arouse his wrath as his willingness to condemn. His colleague Neumann could become indignant at a moment's notice. The university professors who became indignant about the National Socialists were more unpleasant than the National Socialists themselves. Schincke was moving along a quiet river on great floating islands of knowledge and emotion, for the most part kindly disposed toward the passing landscape. In 1934 he did not feel in the least like opposing something that did not directly threaten him, as long as it was only a nuisance. He was the close friend of a number of National Socialists whom he regarded as the paragons who would determine the future. The new education policy pursued by the Minister of Cultural Affairs, himself a philologist, worked to the advantage of both Schincke and the school. The classical section of the Historical Society of the region, of which Schincke was chairman, now received considerable financial grants—it was possible now to stop dabbling and get down to serious study.

For some years Schincke had been doing research on the cultural reforms of Charlemagne. It was more than mere disorientation that motivated his interest in this remote material. He felt there was clear evidence that the quadruple constellation of Charlemagne, Alcuin, Theodulf, and Arn had produced a cultural nucleus of which within thirty short years nothing but fossils remained. It was the brief life of this precious plant to which he wanted to give literary form and whose laws of existence he wanted to describe. The story of the decline of a culture within thirty years was a subject fit for a classical history of ethics. But there was also the fascination of a culture being created out of nothing—for what prior culture could have existed among the barbaric Franks? This was to be the subject of a paper. Granted, he could also have taken contemporary material to develop his ideas, but he did not feel qualified to do this. Moreover, he would have been afraid his ideas might interfere with a still living culture. That was why he preferred to develop his ideas around an example of which there was nothing left to destroy. Another factor was his aversion to topicality, acquired after many years of study, a taboo which he did not regard as binding but to which he nevertheless adhered.

Schincke was now given an assistant for his research; the school acquired a gymnasium which could also double as a concert hall. The assistant was later recalled, however. The favorable attitude adopted by the Government toward classical philology and medieval research proved to be an integral part of the familiar program of pacification: it is best for the mind to occupy itself with ancient or medieval history, this being less dangerous than a preoccupation with the present. Since the end of 1935 and the beginning of 1936, Schincke could be duped no more by the movement and no longer yielded to its blandishments. But what was he to do? By way of contrast with his usual lethargy it could be said that, once roused, he became a menace. But what was the good of being a menace if he was unarmed? After all, he could not cane the object of his wrath, and what he wrote in his diary nobody read. During the 1936 Easter vacation he participated in his last obligatory maneuvers as a captain in the Reserve. He spent his time feeling cold and fighting off stomach upsets. During the final parade of the regiments taking part in the maneuvers outside the town of Qu. he stood to one side of General von Witzleben. One after another the officers riding at the head of the advancing columns of their regiments left their positions, galloped in a semicircle up to the Commander-in-Chief, and saluted. Colonel F. had difficulty in getting his horse, which had adjusted its pace to the other officers' horses, to gallop; at the salute the General coldly dismissed him. While all this was going on Schincke was shivering on the great parade ground where the wind blew unimpeded; like all the others he was mounted on a large horse, not properly equipped for the ordeal. He did not think he would ever forget that terrible day. He observed these maneuvers, and he ceased to believe in the victory of the National Socialists.

During the remainder of April and May there were trips and instructional visits which Schincke had to make as a representative of the Department of Education; in June he was occupied with reorganizing seminar courses for new teachers. In July, complicated libel proceedings between numerous members of the teaching staff had to be headed off; an internal crisis among the faculty, which had been overburdened by the demands of adjusting to the new era. His research took up all his time during August. In September he was given a lectureship at the nearby university; in addition he was put in charge of reorganizing the recently established training center for new teachers. What else could he have done? He was not trained to have a *fait accompli* such as the Third Reich for an enemy.

As the year went on and one activity gave way to the next—had it been a question of pupils one might have called it occupational therapy—Schincke's thoughts continued to flow quietly along. Under the surface, however, the accumulation of minor irritations and observations led to a sudden eruption of antipathy toward the movement which he had hitherto trusted. Many National Socialist colleagues and university professors now found themselves out of favor. He still hoped the fresh tide of 1933 might return on a modified level, if, for example, Hitler ceased to be distracted by foreign policy, but meanwhile he became increasingly hostile to the representatives of this new order. He read fragments from Thomas Mann's *Lotte in Weimar*, brought in from Switzerland, and collected rational explanations for the failure of the National Socialist revolution, which was developing into a state of athletes and patriots. He read a great deal of Nietzsche. This all took place, of course, only in his mind. No one knew anything about his change of attitude. He was not talkative. He did discuss it with his young wife, but he could trust her. Schincke had been brought up to take the separation between idea and reality for granted. He could get along with mental reservations for a long time. An intellectual lives in the past and future just as much as the present, and for him the present is also what is impossible at present, that which has, so to speak, been destroyed by the present; in other words, he can also live in an unborn present, but this requires a strict separation between private and public life. However, the system of channeling essence and reality, his old recipe, did not work with the constant interplay of all spheres of life under this system. Schincke approved, generally speaking, of this aspect of the new system, since he naturally considered it right and proper for lying to be made difficult and truth to be made easy; nevertheless his allergy to the details of this practice continued to grow. The annual rhythm of conferences and assignments—he enjoyed the reputation of a philological luminary—gave him less and less pleasure. Nor could he get around the problem of large numbers. In earlier years he had dealt with the small circle of his school; now he was occupied with hundreds of National Socialists and non-National Socialists, whom he could not love because he virtually did not know them. His wife could not understand why he maintained the separation between his actual functions and his feelings. She believed—just as on principle she believed in the unity of the personality—in gradually adjusting feelings to activities, which after all had been their original state. She thought he should make a greater effort with his feelings. Since, as she saw it, reality could not be changed, she argued in favor of adjusting one's ideas. But Schincke's ideas were firmly anchored, secured by many references and determined by a precise and definite taste on which he claimed to have no influence. The discord between the inner and the outer man, which could be neither maintained nor resolved, caused him physical pain. He would have liked to become ill. He was overburdened. But he did not become ill, he became careless instead. Like the old gentlemen whose verbose opposition to the system he ridiculed, he became garrulous.

In the winter of 1941 Schincke was relieved of his post on account of political utterances concerning the outcome of the war. He was saved from prison by National Socialist friends outside S., whose influence was just sufficient for this. His colleagues Neumann, Reh, and Wirth cut him publicly once the dismissal was announced. Neumann became his successor. The classical section of the Historical Society did not re-elect him. During this time his wife's and his closest friend G., a stage designer at the municipal theater, was forcibly drafted, i.e., the police took him from his apartment after an unsuccessful attempt to run away. G., who had abnormal inclinations, could not possibly endure the constant proximity of rough, normal, sometimes foul-smelling men. A few weeks after he was drafted he suffered a nervous breakdown. He was taken to a military hospital in Dresden. The doctors thought he was shamming, and when G. tried to escape from the hospital he was court-martialed for desertion and shot. His wife, Frau Schincke's bosom friend, after making several last-minute journeys to try and save her husband, took poison when she was told. These weeks, in which he failed to save his friend, led to a temporary separation between Schincke and his wife, who could not believe that her husband was completely powerless, or rather—her actions were seldom dictated by only one motive—could not love a man who, accustomed as he was to an enormous expenditure of mental energy every day for many years, could accomplish nothing in an emergency such as this. She went to Karlsbad Spa, but returned six months later pregnant by an officer of the intelligence corps. Husband and wife agreed on an abortion and after the operation lived together in their suburban villa. All Schincke had to live on was his pension and their ration cards. He found it hard to reduce his standards because he had never been really poor. He could not lead the cramped existence of a retired teacher. He would have gladly gone to the front now, but his application was rejected on grounds of poor physical condition, rejected by a first lieutenant who disliked him and who, like the town's entire upper crust, cut him. Schincke had no connections in the industrial world. The local Party headquarters kept him busy with menial jobs, such as distributing food coupons and checking supplies. There he sat, every month, exposed to public humiliation, doling out food coupons. He tried to get his doctor to declare him medically unfit, but the doctor refused to give him any certificate at all. From time to time he suffered hunger pangs, his large body required large quantities of food. He was overtaxed. His duties as an air raid warden, of which, having no occupation, he was allotted more than most people, prevented him from getting enough sleep. He was in a state in which he was liable to burst into tears if someone spoke to him suddenly. He had long since given up hope that this misery would ever end. He thought of nothing but sabotage, and he made up his mind that, at the next provocation, he would refuse to work and face the consequences. The contempt he was shown from all sides debilitated him and rendered him incapable of continuing his private research. He had lost faith in it. The 20th of July and the subsequent executions frightened him. He would not have believed they would dare kill traitors occupying such exalted positions. He thought the persecution might also affect him, although since 1941 he had been consistently careful, and he was afraid of being mistaken for a member of the Resistance; he was incapable of getting down to any work at all. His wife found it impossible to remain with him and went back to Karlsbad.

The inactivity and the feeling of being treated more and more like an old man had made him so despondent that he regarded the air raid which finally hit S. in March 1945 as a welcome breach of the anathema under which he had been placed. Bombs also fell in the vicinity of Schincke's villa. Schincke emerged from his cellar even before the air raid was over; he was in time to see a group of airplanes flying off. After a brief inspection of his house, which was undamaged, he ran along the disheveled avenue of chestnuts toward the town. On the outskirts Party members were piloting the fleeing inhabitants out of the town. The garrison had left the barracks and were occupying the smoke-filled intersections, which were strewn with broken concrete and splinters and from which one could see a short distance into the burning rows of houses, in the sidestreets. There were onlookers, as if there had been a traffic accident. People carrying homemade preserves hurried through the smoke toward the intersections, in danger from burning housefronts that could collapse at any moment. From one corner to the next Schincke pushed his way toward his old school. He was hoping the school's great cool cellars, which he could not imagine would ever be destroyed, might offer some protection from the almost unbearable heat. The school had been hit by bombs, but only partially destroyed. The pupils, who had been taken unawares by the air raid while they were in class, were waiting in the school yard for instructions from the principal's office. The principal could not decide what to do. Neumann concealed this lack of decision by activity. The telephone service was disrupted and instructions from the school board were unobtainable. After a time messengers arrived from city hall with an evacuation order for the whole school, as the children could not remain in the town. From the Lower Town, consisting of medieval timbered buildings, a wide wall of fire was approaching Cathedral Square. Men were retreating across the square toward the school, where they tried to set up headquarters. Trucks driven by soldiers appeared in the school yard, with orders to remove the pupils. Two hundred people were said to be buried in the air raid shelter at St. Paul's. Principal Neumann gave instructions to the soldiers who reported to him and divided the boys into groups for transportation.

Schincke, who had turned up at first as a mere spectator and out of affection for his old school, was delighted to find himself included in the transportation arrangements. After his wretched years of banishment this seemed to him somehow like a historic moment of national unity, an evocation of the spirit of 1806; he had forgotten that he wanted to do nothing further for these people. Neumann gave him instructions, assigned a private and a driver to him and with their help he was to transport two classes by truck to a specified rendezvous. Thanks to his familiarity with the area, he managed to guide the convoy out of the ruined town along a sandy track beside the river.

As night fell, however, Schincke lost his way. His convoy failed to arrive at the agreed rendezvous, where the school was to assemble and receive further instructions. He gave orders to halt at a spot which was unfamiliar even to him, right next to a barn, no village in sight; a few hundred yards away a highway, unmarked, led past this barn, a path connected the two. The next morning, after spending the night with his pupils in the barn, Schincke felt no urge whatever to get back on the proper route. Not for anything did he want to resume the life of the years 1941 to 1944. He was not prepared to lift a finger for the appalling life he had led during the last few years.

II

My friend Carlton has just returned. I heard the truck coming along the path to the barn. He is talking outside to the boys. I shan't go out. What would I say? I could only say I am glad to see them making friends, and I would feel like my wife when she tries to couple people she is in love with.

I confided in Carlton yesterday. It intoxicates me when he puts his head down to me, his ear close to me.

A reserve officer is supposed to be able to read maps, but I have always been more of a pedagogue, and if it had been possible to be that without at the same time being a reserve officer I would have cheerfully foregone the annual training periods. In any event I have never been much good at map-reading; a fact that has now brought us to quite a different destination from the one planned. If it didn't sound so absurd, I would say that with the mistake we made we have divorced ourselves from events.

Carlton agreed at once. He put a few questions, on which I seized avidly, but these questions were soon settled: I had been expecting questions which would have confirmed the reality of my plan to me. But I grabbed at the questions too hastily (soup bowl upset in eagerness). Carlton let himself be deceived by my plan, for it was only his attentive listening that made it sound so convincing. He said he thought no one could be so convinced of anything unless it were necessary, and that anyone who has so much to say in favor of a plan must himself be convinced of it.

I have never been through anything like it. But I would not want to sacrifice any of the terrible things that happened during the past few days. The air raid (pressed crouching against the cellar steps)—but when I ran through the torn-up town toward my old school what was uppermost in my mind was that I would be able to tell my wife all about it. My realization: a disaster becomes truly terrible only when you no longer feel enriched by the experience. Hence also the old boredom as soon as I am out of danger, the familiar fatigue when I am in the country. I am overcome by boredom as soon as we have settled down in the country. It's not the country that is to blame, it's the change of environment forcing me to leave familiar habits behind. Vague plans, painful, mutilated ideas, inactivity, till there is a new accumulation of habits to bury the daily round in; I would not have thought that the appalling dangers of the last few days would be followed by nothing but the malaise of the city-dweller in rural surroundings.

My heavy body is not suited to days like this. Too much surface that feels cold at night, misses my wife, etc. You have to shake yourself, as you shake a watch or bang a radio (bite your hand) to formulate an idea. A cup of strong coffee would do it, or a refreshing bath. But I can't go and stand under the pump. The icy water would mean a chill. I ought to have started doing it earlier, as N. did, he chops up the ice in the winter and steps down into the freezing hole. But there's no sense in that either, for since the effort to harden himself to the cold takes all my colleague's strength, it doesn't matter whether he hardens himself or not.

Now I have gone outside after all to see why Carlton is talking so much. I did not hide my annoyance, for Carlton has been talking away at these boys, and in my opinion he is just inciting them and making them feel restless. I was disappointed, disappointed that he would rather spend his time with the boys, who have nothing of interest to tell him, than talk to me, who could be instructive about so many things! I felt betrayed and forsaken. It is the same feeling of destructive rage that makes me throw down my glass at a party and leave the room because I can't see my wife but can hear her laughing somewhere. I can hear my wife saying: "What on earth's the matter? Come on, tell me what's wrong! How funny you are etc. . . ."

Presently, I had been following his footsteps outside, Carlton came in to me and sat down beside me, making me feel much better. I stayed where I was, leaning over my frail little table—five narrow boards slapped together—and went on working. If I leaned on it, it would collapse. Its frailty is reminiscent of Desdemona, and I don't suppose anyone has ever said that of a table before.

The flight

Neumann pointed to where the trucks were and kept on talking to me about the route I was to take and the rendezvous with the rest of the school, but after the unexpected greeting, and in my fear that our conversation would suddenly be broken off, I was incapable of taking anything in. Some firefighters stood behind Neumann waiting for orders. He saw them and started to go across to them. He dismissed me with a "my dear Schincke," he oozed charm. He was not really friendly. The strong expression which he gave to his face had been assumed in such a hurry that it didn't fit properly and overflowed its purpose when he said good-by to me with a warmhearted grimace as if we were a couple of pansies. But since this was meaningless, the smile was stuck there, completely out of place, like my sister's hat when it slipped sideways at our mother's funeral. The boys had mounted the trucks, and the older ones, who still remembered me, called out: "Churchill! Churchill!" because since my expulsion, which of course the boys knew all about and which was discussed by their parents, they have no inhibitions about calling me by the name given me at some time or other by the boys. I threaded my way among the various vehicles. They were army trucks, I had two soldiers as my aides: a driver, with colorless hair, and Carlton, who is a private first class and who, when I first saw him, I thought I had seen somewhere before, although it turned out I was mistaken. I asked him: "Everything O.K.?" I thought the children looked tired and over-stimulated, but probably too excited to sleep. They had each been given two blankets. I chatted with them for a bit, and after those hours of terror they were greedy for words and hung over the sides of the truck. I sat down between the driver and the private up front. The memory of how I had lost my head when the first bombs dropped was like a red warning light in front of me. It paralyzes me when someone obeys me. Since I grew up with my mother, who can't give orders, I am used to listening and doing what is expected of me. I get all confused when I find myself in the role of someone who is supposed to give orders. I suspected the driver would take a wrong route out of laziness. I had the impression that he wanted to be independent of the map, in the hope of finding a shorter route. I hadn't quite caught what he and Carlton had been saying to each other, but I gathered they didn't agree—possibly about the direction. So I intervened when the driver seemed about to turn off and ordered him to drive straight on. The road seemed familiar, and since the two soldiers said nothing I took it as a confirmation of my suspicion. Later I realized we had lost our way. That was my fault. I considered taking Carlton into my confidence. But here in the cab the engine was making such a racket that he couldn't understand a word I was saying and told the driver to stop, with the result that I lost my head and asked him for God's sake to drive on.

Hungry, no midday nap: I was cold, and numb from so much happening without a word being uttered. My nerves were making an appalling racket, indistinguishable from the unbearable noise of the engine. My new supply of enthusiasm and sympathy (which we use to warm up things before we take them into our heads) was now all used up. I tried to recall something warming, but memories had become mired. I looked dully at the hairy arms of my companions—the fur of animals: the supply of energy which we use to warm up things before we take them into our heads. We couldn't go on driving like this for ever. So I said:

"It's possible our destination may be changed. I'll let you know."

"Don't you know where we're going?"

"Yes I do, but I have to see first," I replied.

It turned out later that the barn was our destination. I was not sure whether the driver was following my instructions. Both men were looking out for temporary quarters near the road. In my present situation I did not wish to be precise, and I deliberately expressed myself in vague terms, the way you begin to rectify a mistaken idea which you suspect is mistaken by defining it vaguely. The driver with the colorless hair and the insipid pale eyes reminded me of a violinist from my student days. I had chosen a seat in the front row at a concert, where no one normally sat, so as to be nearer the music. This man, from the back row of violinists: "Why don't you sit even closer?" He went on repeating this till I moved to a row further back. I was worried that, if I fell asleep, my head would droop toward the driver's side and, if it rested on his shoulder, might give a quite inappropriate impression of familiarity. Thinking of this I fell fast asleep.

III

Toward morning it got cold in the barn, and as I pulled the blanket around me again in my half-sleep I felt my wife's sleep-warm body against my side. I rolled over, surprised not to be able to find her breast, and found myself looking into the eyes of the child staring at me in horror.

I made some remark or other to break the spell. The merest dab of a new word is enough to make the ideas in these heads immediately fall into new patterns.

It was quite a shock to me, for these children possess the inhuman qualities of their elders; this turning to stone when you brush forbidden territory, in those horrified eyes you are guilty, and not only of touching—of other things, unspecified, much worse.

That morning, because of all the excitement, I had had no bowel movement (I had merely spent a symbolic period of time on the seat in order not to appear different from the others), and accordingly I was very unhappy again. I thought I overheard the boys objecting to the wash cubicle which I had partitioned off for myself in the corner of the barn. I need this last refuge of privacy. We cannot blatantly expose our private habits, if we did we would not be able to hold our own, and Carlton's forbearance toward me, for example, is useless when others find out that we do not wash regularly in this cold weather, or that we do not share other people's inclinations and prefer to follow our own tastes. In this bickering which accompanies my early-morning bodily discomfort, the will is deeply involved. It plays the role of a policeman who hands over the offender to the crowd that wants to lynch him. I was pursued by the vision of a pupil of the graduating class slapping my face while the class howled their approval. I was brooding over this fictitious case—the foam, so to speak, on a restless ocean—when Neumann arrived.

I saw Neumann while I was out for my morning walk, as he turned in from the road, and I tried to head him off to keep him from entering our camp, because of the danger that the boys might overhear us. But he had such a mental picture of the barn as his goal (probably from some way off, possibly even when he started out on his journey) that it was impossible to stop him, nor did he want to talk to me, except for the brief greeting which, as I walked along beside him with my much shorter steps, I did not find as unfriendly as I had expected. But for various reasons this impression was not reliable, partly because he made it clear, by the way he strode silently along, that he would not be "available" till he got to the barn, that he regarded this unscheduled meeting as merely incidental. It must have required an extreme degree of organization to locate us. He had made up his mind to find us even before his termite march began; a march which could only be performed if performed without thinking. Fortunately N. was exhausted by the ordeal.

A train he took to a nearby point was attacked and set on fire by fighter bombers (as one says of a general: three horses were shot from under him).

I had stored the greater part of my will elsewhere. I was in fact not prepared to give in to Neumann. He blamed me for not turning up at the agreed rendezvous. However, after speaking to me as a human being on the day of the air raid he could not now show the contempt with which he had treated me after my dismissal. Neumann is a lean suntanned man, the skin of his face and neck is crisscrossed with lines which form hard stiff creases, and this must mean there is fat beneath the skin, for that cannot be muscle; but it is a very disciplined fat, not what you might call dreamer's fat. I always claim I can see what my wife is thinking: she thinks with her shoulders, her arms, her whole body. N. doesn't do that. He uses the logic springing from his head to riddle his environment, but he does not really grasp it. My incompetence he could forgive; but that I was opposed on principle to leaving this place was something he could not understand. I tried to divert his attention by talking about what was likely to happen on the Oder and Rhine fronts. He had to admit that the Oder front had probably already collapsed. N. tried to brush away this conversation, which I had spread over him like a net, but the subject was well chosen. Again and again I find it is the magic of words which is my best weapon; a weapon which does not fail me even with someone like N., who is only partially susceptible, but I wouldn't be able to ensnare him in symbols. After a time, when I felt equal to it again, I resumed the conversation about our evacuation. I took as my main argument the fact that for the time being we were safe here. N. had to admit that the boys assembled at the rendezvous had already been listed in the rolls, that their camp was known to all the authorities and in all probability they would be recruited for defense purposes. I enumerated many other reasons for my standpoint, perhaps not quite as convincing. I could not give in, if only because, even if I gave in now, it would still mean a severe punishment and a denunciation by N. Like Wallenstein, I had already gone too far, in a kind of intoxication with my victory over this man who had made my life a misery for four years and now proved incompetent in a simple dialogue. I cited the case of my grandfather who, when his strength for all else failed, took to breeding sheep. He lived for them, he mashed potatoes for them, cut the bad places out of the potatoes before feeding them to the sheep, later he slaughtered the sheep. Also: that we had to cultivate the boys like valuable trees—a rare plant—and must not expose them to destruction, for every boy is unique, even though they tend to look alike. It was really the incompetence of the teachers that made them all look alike. He wouldn't admit this. I attacked him at another point: in Dresden, after Luther's death, the traditional exorcism of the Devil at baptism was to be abolished. A butcher stood behind the priest and threatened to bring his ax down on him if he did not drive the Devil out of his infant son. Neumann did not think this proved anything since reason ultimately opposed driving out the Devil. Not when the butcher is standing behind you, I replied. Carlton still did not turn up. I sent someone to look for him. Right to the end I believed the decision would be made on the field of argument. But N. had got an idea into his head: he had decided I didn't want to join the last-ditch stand. I got Carlton to drive him to the station, which was several miles away, and gave N. a bottle of cognac as a parting gift, although I could certainly have put it to better use than he could, for he will only give it away.

I wandered around some more for a while, the conversation had made me restless. Now that I can do so without jeopardizing the issue, I find Neumann's attitude admirable. My thoughts seldom fit what I want to say. Like the Polish miners' families, who multiply to such an extent during the long journey from their native country to the Rhineland that the houses which have been prepared for the families are no longer big enough, my similes are no longer big enough for my rapidly multiplying thoughts, although only a moment ago they were. Respect for humanity and scholarship prevents people like

Carlton or N. from casually knocking over the frail thought-structures we are able to offer them. They are not really thought-structures, they are secret symbols which sound like nonsense, I am now about to give another simile: they are the echo-sounding devices I need in order to plumb my real meaning.

My Dearest,

I hope you're not getting into too much mischief in Karlsbad. I don't say this because you're my wife, for in these troubled times such an attitude is pretty irrelevant. Nor do I wish to dress up in biological disguise something which is morally obsolete: that it would be better for your health, for instance, and for your complexion, if you exercised some restraint. Oh well, there's really no point in my telling you all this. The distance between us is more than I can bear. The alleged dangers which threaten you and which my jealousy invents are gigantic. Why did you have to go to that wretched Karlsbad again? Haven't I warned you that your lust for life is bound to drive you to disaster? With life as complicated as it is for us all nowadays, you can't simply start living and think everything's going to be all right. I don't mean to say Nature is our enemy, but I believe that you in your way have just as little notion of how to get along with yourself as I have in mine. You can't run wide-eyed to meet your happiness. Be careful how you pick your adventures. But what am I worrying about, maybe you really are only taking the cure, though I find that hard to imagine!

When we went to the station, the two of us, and we were at a loss for words before we said good-by, we had both stopped talking, wasn't our quarrel over by then? How often have we quarreled like that, and our tears were the beginning of an embrace! Wasn't everything all right again as we sat in the station restaurant with our farewell drink? I can't believe those were the final words of our marriage, just because you might be silly enough to rush headlong into disaster. You only have to make friends with one of those big brutes who are probably lying around in Karlsbad convalescing and watching their end approach, one way or another. You leave your hotel in the morning, walk through the park. The eyes of the less seriously wounded follow you from countless hotel windows. In the evening you are simply incapable of resisting the words and hints, the pleas. Your imagination is highly inflammable, and you are too much alive to offer any resistance. You become hopelessly involved, your head full of hopes of something undefined, something for which in this way it is surely too late now. The Czechs watch you and will include you in their revenge. What are you hoping for? What have you been looking for all these war years? You know as well as I do that you never find anything in these little adventures. I believe we are all in the grip of that solemn feeling which this war has spread among us; a deceptive feeling which seems to bring our ideals within our reach. Must something even greater emerge when the great soap-bubble of war bursts? Why didn't you stay with me? I didn't want to persuade you not to go because I was hoping that in a moment of magnanimity you would say: Shall I go or shan't I? Let the train go without me, you might have said. But the noise inside you, your lack of confidence in me, your doubts as to whether I am still your ideal or whether I'm not one of your disappointments which you shed like a dress that hasn't brought you any luck! And yet maybe you want to spare your ideal, give me a respite till I've got hold of myself again?

How often have your Don Juans in Karlsbad, whom I envy and hate, disappointed you when they have tried out their newly won life-force on you? But do you shed them? Dutifully you carry your beautiful sensuality year after year to market. If you were here and I could hold you in my arms I would not be so suspicious. You are too good-natured, too optimistic, much too unsuspecting—even though you suspect me. You are fooled, you think there are people who know you as I know you. When you are looking for something difficult to learn, when you are looking for something new which might work a miracle, when you press yourself against me and caress me because you would like to find out more about miracles. Ambitious and corruptible through your skin, but also incorruptible through your skin, which never forgets a disappointment. I can't stand our being so far apart, otherwise I wouldn't be writing all this; if I could only touch you I would know you are safe. The men you are going around with now will exploit you and pass you on from one to the other. And when the Russians arrive you will be surprised because those same men will trade you for food or a bicycle. I know I'm talking nonsense, but I can't stand our being so far apart, it seems unnatural. Why didn't you stay with me? A streak of generosity, the kind you admire in yourself, just one second, enough for you to say: Well, should I stay?

This letter, like a number of others, could not, of course, be mailed by Schincke where he was. He hesitated to give the letter to Neumann, who might have been able to mail it somewhere; besides, when Neumann turned up the letter was still only a torso. And he had no intention of asking Carlton to mail it, although Carlton might have found an opportunity. Moreover, it was doubtful whether the mail was still getting through to Karlsbad. Nor was Schincke sure how his wife would react to this letter, he knew what she was thinking when he could look at her, but he was helpless when he knew she was far away. So Schincke left the letter among his papers which were gradually accumulating here.

IV

Carlton told me there is a big estate near by. It is situated in the hills we can see from the barn. Next to the manor house are the houses for the farm laborers, two great wings built of brick, next to them the huts for the Polish women laborers and the Russian prisoners. Carlton has made contact with the people who run the estate. He maintains he knows the lady of the manor personally, but I regard this as an attempt to impress me. To make his conquest sound more believable he says he has ceased to find any pleasure in this woman. (But he has found out, so he says, that he can use this woman for our purposes, and that makes up for it. He doesn't have to love her, he says, he just has to get something out of it.)

He has brought me two volumes of Montaigne bound in red morocco. I had hinted he might take a look in the toilets, reading matter was often left lying around there. Now he has brought along these dark-red beauties, they made their appearance just as I was emerging, invigorated, from my midday nap: at the most receptive moment of the day. I wanted to kiss him on the lips, but it misfired because he tried to shake me off. He allows me to do many unusual things. Moreover, he has brought me a list of all the members of the First Infantry Guard Regiment for the years 1904 and 1905. Now I can pore over all those glorious names.

The children are being taken to the manor house for a bath. This has to be done at night, of course. I have prepared myself for this nocturnal adventure by an invigorating sleep, for which I lay down after sunset. This sleep before a party or a tour of the dance halls and night clubs: you wake up with lips so full of blood you could cut right into them and the crimson blood would come spurting out in a great arc. Your body feels like a mere husk for this pulsating blood, like the skin of a balloon. I took my turgid lips like an engorged cox-comb to Carlton, who was just about to start up the truck, but there seemed to be some hitch. I was instantly seized with that old fear that the adventure might not take place; a reflex which has always prevented me from running any risk before a party or an adventure, whether it was putting on any clothes except the ones I can count on to always bring me luck, or asking Carlton why he couldn't get the truck started by kicking it, as I had seen him do before. I simply can't think why I didn't love this reliable beast right from the beginning, with its great headlights up front, although they are only visi-ble through narrow slits. It is much easier to control than horses, which have always seemed uncanny to me with their housewives' eyes. You can't get as fond of them as you can of this machine when it starts rattling after a few bangs and kicks. The headlights are turned on, Carlton happens to touch the horn, and the truck makes a sound like a dog that interprets even its master's involuntary movements as orders.

For some reason or other I had expected us to be received at the estate with hurricane lamps, but then of course we would not have had to come at night. I am inclined to regard caution as a refinement of pleasure, and was surprised when I found myself actually in danger here, for Carlton hissed at me when I got out and was about to speak to the boys. Lights were still burning in the servants' quarters, so we had to stop the noisy truck some distance from the main house, unload our freight quietly and take it to a rear entrance of the house, where a maid was waiting for us.

Here I was, like in the campaign in France. I found my way to the paneled library of the manor. Carlton tried to usher me out of this library, because he said it might be dangerous if lights were seen. I must admit I had turned on all the lights as if for a party (the mistress of the house ought to consider Carlton sufficient recompense for the increase in the light bill). However, I was able to point out that the blinds were drawn and that the owner could suddenly decide she wanted something to read just as easily as I could. At this stage I still believed Carlton really did know the owner and that for this reason a good deal was permitted which would otherwise not be permitted in a strange house. Carlton, who knew better but who is easy-going by nature, gave in and left me in the library.

I had already picked out several books and arranged them around me. So there I was, sitting among my treasures, when the mistress of the house walked in, I rose courteously and, as one does when getting up from one's chair to greet a visitor, a little stiffly, I kissed her hand and introduced myself a little stiffly too. I alluded to my friend Carlton, but she did not react to this, which meant that I spoke several sentences into a void. But it was not out of the question for me to get this woman to like me, since Carlton, as I well knew, had arrived at such and such a point. She offered me some cognac. I also accepted a cigarette. She held a cigarette with a charming gesture slightly away from herself while she poured the cognac. The owner seemed to be surprised at our visit rather than prepared for it. We had reached the vicinity of the cognac again before it became evident that she had not invited us at all.

Despite all my democratic ideals—and the important thing after all is to see that the masses share in our cultural heritage, and failure to solve the problem of the masses is the thing I blame National Socialism for in my heart of hearts—whenever

I find myself with people of my own kind, i.e., members of the élite—and how much more does this apply in lonely rural surroundings!—I am overwhelmed by happiness, a sense of belonging, which I would not care to be deprived of and which I would strive to salvage in a new era, if such salvaging were possible (and there were a new era). Among equals everything is permissible: the old game of pretense, the fluctuation between the highest breeding and animal bodies; I know that is all out of date and bad, but for an hour it held me spellbound again. This woman, whose husband was in command of a regiment somewhere in Croatia, even supposing he were still alive, this woman who offered me cognac that got under my skin and spread warmth inside me while her words were warming me outside, gave me books, at least she said I could take along any of the books I had chosen. It is only natural that I felt like an officer in enemy country, since the mood of this conversation matched the age of bygone wars.

V

The high-pitched humming of the little motor approaching from the road, like a bloodthirsty insect. Sensing danger when the sound suddenly ceased, I had gone out to our sentry. On the way there I suddenly saw the farmer, as if he had shot up out of the ground, this is the order in which I received my impression of him: old green hat, clumping boots, little brown eyes, an armband.

"Heil 'tler."

"Heil Hitler," I replied and invited him to come along for a drink: Let's have a drink first, shall we? The farmer demanded to see my papers. I did not understand right away what he wanted, and these moments were wasted for my de-

liberations, since he took my failure to understand for evasion.
I gave him what I had on me: pension card, monthly streetcar
pass with photo. In the interval that followed, while the
farmer studied the documents, I said we had been bombed out
and ordered to come here. Some boys came running up, and I
sent a few of them off to get Carlton. The farmer looked up
puzzled from his papers.

"You don't seem to have any proper identification," he
said, handing me back the papers. He asked me some more
questions, and I was glad about this, for it seemed to me that if
we could only talk long enough I was bound to be able to un-
thaw him. I wanted to show him everything. I did not leave
my farmer's side for an instant, I kept on talking to him in per-
suasive tones, the way my wife has heard me do whenever I
am involved with the police or anything really dangerous. I
laid mines, so to speak, I produced so many reasons why it was
lawful and necessary for us to remain here that if he tried to
get his thoughts back on the old track they were bound to step
on these mines and be thrown off the track. I had the feeling
we might be able to win the farmer round. The farmer said:
"Please order all the members of your party to assemble here."

"And what's going to happen to the children?"

He did not answer; instead he sat down by my table.
Apart from turning his thick skull a couple of inches, he gave
no sign of life. I once heard of a farmer who lost his way in his
fields when he was drunk and, because he persisted with his
drinking movements, swallowed so much earth that he died. I
saw Carlton, the boys. The sense of gratitude and the fresh
wave of assurance when I saw them come in. It was the same
deceptive feeling of security as I had had that time when I
opened the front door and the four Brownshirts approached
and I saw the taxi driver turn his cab round and come back
again so that the Brownshirts stopped approaching. But just as

the taxi driver, in spite of some shouting back and forth with the Brownshirts, could not protect me, and one of the Storm Troopers managed to get his foot in the door and nab me in the hall, so Carlton's protection failed me here too.

"I've been arrested, Carlton," I called out to him. "The children are being taken away!"

But by now the farmer had come to life, he went over to Carlton and did the same as he had with me.

"Your identity papers, please," etc.

All the boys had arrived by this time, the farmer ordered them to form ranks of three and, since he did not trust me and Carlton, put the boys Pichota and Hartmann in command. They immediately set about dividing the boys up into ranks of three. I had the terrible feeling that everything was slipping through my fingers.

"What's going to happen to the children?" I asked again, in such a loud voice that the farmer looked round. Carlton did nothing. The organizing of the boys took some time. I tried to catch Hartmann's and Pichota's eyes, but they avoided mine, they obeyed the one who had entrusted them with this important responsibility. Only a few of the smaller boys seemed to me to have kept a natural sense of what was right and proper. I tried to communicate with them by signs. They looked across at me uncertainly, not knowing what to make of my signs. Then a few of the boys who had not yet been split up into ranks actually ran out toward the road. The farmer, not grasping what was happening but sensing danger, drew his pistol and shouted: "Stop!" But he could not shoot because we were on top of him. The boys' ranks broke up.

When we got off him (like dogs who have got their teeth into an enemy dog), he stood up, his green hat rather battered, a gaping wound in his face. Without a word he walked over to his motorbike, blood dripping, spattering his jacket, while we stayed right where we were so as not to undermine our victory. He picked up his bike, an ordinary bicycle to which he had attached an auxiliary motor, and pushed it toward the road, walking like a man who is retreating but doesn't want to show he has cause to retreat. For quite a while we could hear the malevolent throbbing of the auxiliary motor driving his bike up the hill.

VI

Toward evening armored vehicles and army transport trucks appeared on the road going past our hideout, three abreast and pulling cannons, they were making for the hills. Their headlights were switched off, the only sounds were the deep roar and the clanking of treads from the road. After a time the column came to a standstill, orders were shouted, some vehicles tried to move on by pulling out sideways across the field. Perhaps they were afraid that fighter planes might recognize the vehicles in the dusk with night binoculars? Presently a military staff gathered round an officer a little way off the road, and dispatch riders were sent out from this command post.

On my evening walk, accompanied by some of the boys, I went as far as the convoy. From one of the officers' cars came the sound of music. I could not identify it right off. I told the boys who were with me to listen closely, and spoke sharply to them when they gave no immediate sign of listening, the way one speaks sharply to someone who refuses a piece of bread in times of dire shortage. There is nothing more annoying than a lack of intuitive awareness.

The musical presence which had brought me happiness

here in my exile in the country (rather like being exiled to the Black Sea), lasted only a moment. The driver of the vehicle, who had been talking to the other drivers, came over to us. I tried to head him off as he approached the car and make him realize the beauty of the music before he could turn it off. He looked up in surprise from his wordless trot. He walked round me, as I was standing in his way. I was therefore several paces away from the vehicle and could not prevent him from reaching inside. I said: "Please don't turn off the music for a moment," etc., but he had already found another station. The soldier remained standing near us but looked over at us with a not unfriendly expression.

VII

Yesterday we could hear cannons booming from the west during the day. Some of the vehicles on the road tried to reach the hills but were discovered by fighter planes. Carlton has been gone for two days. He is full of projects, restless as a gambler, a threat to our safety. Nevertheless I look for him, toward the road—until I thought, he won't come for sure if I keep looking, so I went back, feeling certain he had already returned to the barn, but I did not find him there.

I have sent out search parties to look for Carlton.

Carlton has been hanged. From the curving bough of a pine tree. Chalk marks on the soles of his shoes, like the ones foresters make on trees.

I have been to see the lady of the manor because I have to talk to someone. But she received me with such exceptional warmth that I soon found myself in a false situation. I kept on chatting, not knowing how to break out of this diabolical circle. From my full heart, as if from a full stomach, I suggested we call each other by first names. The sudden intimacy brought my emotions to the surface and I could have talked about Carlton's black tongue, but just then she made some witty remark, I don't remember now what it was—temporary mental anesthesia brought on by the joke, the result was we lapsed again into a warm, unreal tone of voice, as if we were saying good-by, while we finished our drinks, until she let me out into the night, and then she could not refrain from saying my first name, which had been on the tip of her tongue: Eberhard.

VIII

Shoals of silver fish with bloody heads: all day long they fly back and forth over the road. Not a vehicle escapes their notice. I am completely out of touch with the situation. I find all this terribly exciting although I ought really to see the danger, but I quite like the danger, I ought really to be worrying about my safety and that of my pupils, but actually all I want to do is start teaching again.

Dream No. 1
I have been dancing all night with a very short little hunchbacked man, I have to bend right down to him, he is wearing riding breeches. Feel a great revulsion, but am afraid that to refuse him would be harmful to me.

Dead mouth, drawn tightly together like a miser's purse (André Gide). All day long I have been fluctuating between two quotations which are meaningless to me but which I can't get out of my head:

1. Appropinquante morte animus multo est divinior (Cicero, *De Divinatione*, I, 63).

2. A man sentenced to death says: Light! An immense quantity of light, thanks be to God! Another man turns his food bowl upside down over his head and says: Let's go! We must play the fool to the very end.

Dream No. 2

Practice alert! We are taken out onto an open square where a guillotine has been erected. We are told this is merely a trial run to establish the height of our necks so that, in the event of an execution, we could be correctly laid out on the plank and the whole procedure would be carried out more quickly. In place of the guillotine blade a typewriter ribbon has been stretched across the frame. The whole thing looks like a fretsaw, only that instead of the saw blade there is a typewriter ribbon, and when this drops it will mark the exact point of impact. They stand us up there in turn. I don't trust it at all, I suspect they're going to secretly exchange the ribbon for a blade. I have just been fastened into position when I look up. And there I see, the shining blade of an ax. I scream: "There!"

IX

In the case of the farmer, at least I was immediately aware of his malevolence. I am not cut out for situations like this. I am really no more restless than at any other time, probably I lack a proper grasp of the situation, but what am I supposed to do? Perhaps I used to have the necessary fear, distributed through my life to date? I could not claim to be exercising my mind since there has been this danger. One ought to be able to use one's brain now, but I cannot really relate to danger. What use is my head to me now if they can bash it in at any moment? It must be better protected; actually we can divide the whole human mind up into an efficiently working brain, like Carlton's, although this didn't help him, and measures for protecting this brain. But how am I to explain this to someone who believes in the power of the intellect? Hanging from that tree, and his tongue! Not a thing one can do, not a thing: like two logs, those legs. I could have touched them. Would never have dared do such a thing when he was alive. But seeing him hanging there like that, it's really impossible to think of any reason why I didn't. Maybe we had better leave?

I came on the officer unawares while he was talking to the boys. As I approach, silence on the part of the boys and the officer, as if I had surprised a pair of lovers. I asked the officer if I could speak privately to him, regardless of whatever he wanted with the boys. He tried to make excuses and did not want to follow me into the barn, but after my short midday nap I was like a recharged battery. My suspicion that he wanted to talk the boys into joining a trench-digging detail proved to be correct. I showed him the weapon I had taken from the farmer. There were no vehicles to be seen on the road at this time.

I allowed him to pick up the bicycle on which he had ridden here and wheel it to the road. He was no coward. As he rode off I fired a bullet after him which crashed into the trees lining the highway.

Guards have been posted while we start to work. The guards keep us informed about the traffic on the highway. The meaning of the last few days cannot be: live dangerously; if only because there is the possibility we shall not survive the danger. I break off, the guards signal. The sound of engines comes up the road.

X

Et volat saepius carta caritatis alis pennata implens officium linguae.

78:119,25

In a letter to Theodulf of Orléans, Alcuin gives the following definition: *memor esto sacerdotalis dignitatis linguam caelestis esse clavem imperii et clarissimam Christi tubam. Quapropter ne sileas, ne taceas, ne formides loqui.*

225:368,29

Loqui is therefore a spiritual duty and corresponds to priestly dignity. Respect for the word involves obligation toward the word on the part of the priest. Hence the recurrent admonition to speak: *nolite tacere.*

225:413,4

Silentium in sacerdote pernicies est populi. Loqui is justified not as an arbitrary communication but by its inherent goal: it is the key to *imperium regni caelestis.*

113:164,32

Rationalis intellegentia is the organ in which *discere* has its seat and at which *docere* is aimed. It is the natural property of man. Mention has already been made of the qualifying *rationalis* in Alcuin.

113:164,34

Lingua: seat of *loqui* and thus of *docere*, implies *rationalis intellegentia; cor* on the other hand is the organ of reception of *gratia*, the seat of *religio*. In *cor* and *intellegentia* we have a further example of those dual unities which so frequently mark style and thought of the sources of that time.

Sapientia forms a kind of synthesis of *intellegentia* and *cor*. It is *sapientia* which triumphs over the state of *rudis* as it has been adopted as a term from the works of St. Augustine (i.e., as *catechizandus*), and as it is understood in the circumstances and conditions of the eighth century.

34:75,24

Alcuin is concerned for the welfare of his pupils and does all he can for them. In a letter to Adalhard of Corbie he begs him to intercede with Charlemagne to permit his pupil Bernarius to return from the world to his monastery *Lérins*.

There is a further example of a dispute on behalf of pupils, in this case, however, with a more "official" background and more serious consequences. It leads to a temporary breach between Alcuin and Theodulf of Orléans, and even to a severe reprimand from Emperor Charlemagne.

During the day Schincke was now at work again on his paper on the cultural reforms of the Carolingian empire, which he had started planning in 1932 and writing in 1934. He realized that, like resuming teaching, this could be an inappropriate reaction to events and the present situation; but what reaction was to be expected from him? The very fact that it was an emergency made him cling instinctively to what he knew. What else could he have done? Plot a revolution? He sensed that the turning-point he had been waiting for since 1933 was now past, and that this time there had been no change either. He was glad to be able to safeguard the remnant of good will which he still possessed by investing it here in literary productivity. Instinctively he moved toward this opportunity: to make a new beginning with the boys in his care. The following day, after being denounced by the farmer whom he had wounded and who came from a near-by village, Schincke was arrested by a mobile military court. The boys were rounded up and taken to neighboring farms. Schincke was taken to the nearest large town. It was while he was there, separated from his pupils, that he was liberated.

Sergeant Major
Hans Peickert

The messenger in the service of the last Reich Chancellor but one before Hitler from 1928 to 1933 was called Hans Peickert. In later years he advanced to sergeant major. His parents and ancestors had been hardly more than serfs on some landed estates in West Prussia. At the age of twenty Peickert went to Berlin and entered the service of the said Herr von P. The cornucopia of rich gifts offered by politics and the new era was spilling its contents over the Conservatives, who had stood fast in troubled times. As a messenger Peickert became part of his master's intricate communications network. The new opulence coming after the age-old Prussian shabbiness, although it only benefited his master, convinced Peickert of the dawning of a new era.

The nationalist Right's methods of government

After the downfall of the monarchy, the nationalist Right looked on the Germany that remained as a kind of large fief to be divided up. Friends and respected enemies joined together to form a powerful right wing. In the Baltic provinces, in Berlin, in rebellious Saxony, in Bavaria, this right wing quickly made the obdurate see reason. With animal persistence the right wing built a façade of duty. Under this guise of duty it set out to trap men.

Peickert trapped since birth

West Prussia had offered no opportunity for Peickert. But in von P.'s service there was no opportunity for him either. Peickert's status excluded him from sharing in the political spoils. Since working for his master required all Peickert's energies, it was really immaterial whether he worked for this one master or for many masters in West Prussia. The only thing he had control over was his girl friend Magda S. In 1932 he attempted to make her work for him on the streets. As a result he was reported to the police. Von P. warned him. Soon after that von P. joined Hitler's cabinet. There were signs that his downfall was imminent. Peickert thought this was the moment to get away from his master. He asked to be allowed to join the Army.

The statesman refused to recognize his imminent downfall

Von P., who had just been appointed Hitler's Vice Chancellor, ordered Peickert to remain. Time and again von P. tried in his speeches and conversations to salvage something for himself and his friends. After losing his post as Vice Chancellor in 1934 he tried at least to retain his substitute post as German ambassador in Vienna. The annexation of Austria did away with von P.'s ambassadorial post. One of von P.'s closest collaborators was shot. At the end of 1934 Peickert was accepted as a recruit in the German Army.

II

After leaving von P.'s service, Peickert was filled with new hope. The elimination of the old masters now seemed to Peickert to betoken the extension of the cornucopia to all the faithful. In the Army he had advanced in 1935 from recruit to private, in 1936 from private to private first class, in 1938 from private first class to corporal. With the expansion of the Army immediately before the outbreak of war he made the leap to sergeant. During the first year of the war he became a sergeant major. This gradual rise from someone who is of no importance whatever with very little pay, to someone who is of slightly more importance with a little more pay, did not correspond to Peickert's idea of increasing the scope of his opportunities. He now put his hopes in the war. The war was supposed to expand the *Lebensraum* of the German people. Peickert pictured this as having a wide application.

War conducted according to prison regulations

In Peickert's life so far there had been nothing but disappointment. The urge to imitate his parents, to obey the lord of the manor, had betrayed him; no one gave him credit for this good intention or any derivative of it. The urge to be popular in school did him no good. His hopes in his great master in Berlin deceived him, since his master merely exploited him. But his hopes in the National Socialists deceived him too, for his gradual advancement in the Army, the weapons and equipment, the promise of improved accommodation after the war, the prospect of a chance to increase his knowledge at a military school, offered no prospect of the radical change Peickert was seeking. Finally the war itself was a bitter disappointment. The troops marching into Poland were disciplined. Soldiers found looting were frequently shot. The shooting of this or that enemy or of impertinent civilians brought no change in the overall situation. In France things were much the same.

Pearls of wisdom, store of childhood memories

Use your head where it does the most good.
Keep under cover and sit it out.
Click goes the brain, yackety yack goes the billygoat.
First you're cheated, then you lie, you've smartened up.
Let the kike have it in the schnoz.
Don't ask why, say that's why.
Go fly a kite.
That's that.

Memory: Big holiday when the county council gave official permission for the storming of the pharmacy in S., which had been proved to be handling contaminated drugs. Pots of ointment smashed against the walls. Fire broke out later on in the so-called laboratory.

Childhood memories of the pregnant housekeeper at the manor: the local doctor had attempted to turn the child around in the woman's belly as it was lying incorrectly. Injuries had resulted. All one Christmas this woman lay bleeding to death on a stretcher in the laundry room (the birth was supposed to be kept a secret). The bleeding exhausted the woman more and more. Yawning. Fear, as the blood ran out.

Lullaby:

Trickle, trickle, dribble drip.

A nasty gash, beyond a doubt
Dolly's gone and hurt herself,
    All the sawdust's running out.

Peickert's appearance

Deep chest, short neck: well suited for a resonant voice. The lower part of his body solidly built. Face with no special features: nervous areas around the temples, dun-colored hair; hard, calloused lips, or rather: shutting apparatus. No fixed habits: like many emigrants from what used to be Central Europe (unlike farmers or peasants), not settled—hard to get hold of, a shell with many uses: but housing a strong desire for expansion. This figure was encased in the smart uniform of a sergeant major with a lanyard. His cap was pinched right and left at the front and was too small for his head, he wore it at a slight angle. Raucous bark on duty, modulated transmitter in private, i.e., in business.

Special type of intelligence

He was obsessed with the idea of rousing the movement "yes" in Lieutenant Tacke's face (sensation; sign; flaring up of the old promise: good). Peickert's language, his whole body in fact, was attuned to that particular form of transmission which would prompt Tacke's reaction. Without consideration for truthful utterance, consequences, or harm, Peickert extracted material from his environment, re-minted it, re-forged it, and poured it into this one purpose: to summon understanding in Tacke's face. Bankrupt, entangled in untenable utterances and promises, in a state of inner turmoil, Peickert took leave of his superior.

Business training

At school Peickert bartered stolen food for true confession and adventure stories. He bartered his talents for Herr von P.'s favor, which was of no use to him. He bartered his girl friend so the charge of procuring would be dropped. He bartered his life expectancy, in a certain sense his very life, for the opportunity of advancement in the Army. If Peickert had had children, they might have achieved the leap to still greater barter status, the leap to an academic career for example. They could never have become members of the upper class. Peickert did not want to have children with an academic career; as things stood now he did not want any children at all just yet, he wanted to live himself.

Duty and life

Peickert spent the summer of 1940 in France. His division was resting up in Lille, France. In Metz, Hans Peickert met Angélique Danatier, who later became his fiancée. As soon as he could exert sufficient power over her, he offered her services to officers at the garrisons of Lille, Metz, Montmédie, and Rheims. He also trafficked in weapons, English cigarettes, and leave passes, as well as a variety of commissariat goods. On duty Peickert was the perfect image of a German sergeant major.

III

The garrison town of Lille in France lies in a valley. Behind the railway district lie the barracks, already used to quarter German troops during World War I. However, some private houses had also been requisitioned in Lille for billeting purposes. One of these houses, the Villa Hébert, situated on the road leading out of the city toward the southeast, had been allocated to Sergeant Major Peickert and his staff. In the house next door on the right lived the French mayor appointed by the occupying forces, the property on the left was occupied by counterintelligence men. Peickert's duties in Lille consisted of being in charge of a training unit, the supervision of a number of local factories, and conducting some of the Lille headquarters' correspondence. Moreover, as a favor Peickert had taken over the temporary running of an antiaircraft battery near Lille that was without a quartermaster. Except for the times when he was away on official duty, the day began for Peickert at six A.M. with company inspection. This was followed by the hoisting of the flag. Shortly before seven Peickert appeared at the office of the antiaircraft battery where he took care of some of the correspondence. At nine A.M. every fourth day Peickert reported to the commandant, every sixth day to the Lille counterintelligence headquarters (next door), as well as to army and air force units in Lille where he had friends. From eleven to two he inspected the work of the training unit and had lunch. From three to six he attended to correspondence. At six o'clock Peickert usually went off duty.

The performance of his duties allowed of numerous variations. For example, by doing some of his work ahead of time, the hours allotted to correspondence between seven and nine in the morning and three and six in the afternoon could be saved. For the flag-hoisting and company inspection, a sergeant was sufficient every second and third day. Inspection of the training unit's work could be spun out. Peickert had the reputation of deserving support. If he had been away from his unit for a week, no one would have noticed; in 1940 and 1941 Peickert made no trip that took him away from the garrison for more than two and a half days. He had 620 men and twelve noncoms under him. In the Villa Hébert his immediate subordinates were Sergeants Freyer and Müller-Segeberg.

Business report for 1940, up to the crisis of the winter of 1941/42

From July 1940 Peickert's business projects, as they existed at a level below the strict performance of his duties, were as follows:

Oct.	Sale of weapons	4,000.00
	English cigarettes	300.00
	Payments from Angélique and Marika	800.00
	Profit on one lot nylons to Halberstadt, Oschersleben and Wernigerode; 10% commission	1,200.00
	Commissariat goods, profit	600.00
	Miscellaneous	300.00
	Plus pay (cash)	138.00
		RM. 7,338.00

		REICHSMARK
July	Payments from Angélique	120.00
	Plus pay (cash)	138.00
		RM. 258.00

August/Sept.	Payments from Angélique	300.00
	Payments from Marika G., from mid-Sept.	280.00
	Profit on commissariat goods, food and drink	100.00
	Plus pay (cash)	276.00
	Maneuver allowance	32.00
		RM. 988.00

The year from November 1940 to November 1941 could be called his first fiscal year. November 1940 saw the establishment of business connections with Army Command Areas IV and VI. The November successes were followed by a trip to former Poland with the aim of buying up some property near Posen. In January Peickert bought a property in Graudenz. He established his residence in this town. Peickert's peripheral activities now included: commission on Angélique's and Marika's earnings; trading in lumber, trading in gasoline, small-arms trafficking, tobacco, commissariat goods. That year brought in 43,000 marks cash, a property worth 17,000 marks, as well as a number of prospects for the future. Peickert sensed the approaching crisis of the winter of 1941. From November 1941 until February 1942 he did no business, since he was afraid of large-scale controls and inspection of supplies behind the lines sparked by the winter's disasters on the Eastern front. He waited, so to speak, until the extent of the danger became clear.

Motto: a joy to live
A well-known right-wing author said: It is a joy to live! On the other hand the song says: Who joy desires, who joy selects, his earthly lot will e'er be pain; who ne'er desires nor chooses joy, his earthly lot will ne'er be pain. Peickert hoped his lot would "ne'er be pain." That was why he did not make a beeline for joy. It gave him quite a sense of satisfaction to play hamster this winter of the war 1941/42, i.e., to have sufficient reserves on hand to guard against any contingency. But there was also some joy, as a by-product. Unforgettable, the twilight mood of the first air raids on Berlin, spent in the zoo air raid shelter. Unforgettable, too, the quick trip on December 31, 1941, to Wannsee. Predated files passed on to superiors on the preceding day seemed to leave no doubt that Peickert was carrying out his duties in Lille.

Achievements of the Reich railways

Until well into the summer of 1942 the train schedules throughout Western Germany as well as in France remained reasonably reliable. Delays were announced with up to thirty-six hours' notice and could be ascertained by telephone at a distance of four to six hundred miles. Now and again the airport administration would offer Peickert a seat in a fighter plane that happened to be making a quick trip. The Balkans, which were to become very important to Peickert in 1942, could only be reached by plane. On one occasion Peickert bartered a trainload of gasoline that was on its way from a Stettin refinery to Kielce and was threatened with inspection and line disruption for a much smaller troop transport on a private siding in Central Germany.

Sense of fear

Peickert carried two wallets with amounts ranging from 600 to 1,000 marks on him whether he was traveling or not. When his reserves dropped below 600 marks he felt afraid. A sense of insecurity paralyzed him, making him incapable of decision but at the same time suspicious of decisions that might be the right ones, since he was afraid of wrong decisions made in a panic. On the other hand, his suspicions increased his sense of fear. Hence the constant provision for the future in the form of numerous wallets, some of which were carefully concealed.

Stalingrad

The annihilation of the Sixth Army before Christmas 1942 and in the dark days of January 1943 threw a shadow over everything going on in Germany at that time. It also gave Peickert's affairs a kind of consecration, an atmosphere of imminent danger, which Peickert found agreeable because it reflected the proportion of his state of fear better than holidays, time at the beach, special announcements, promotion, or preparations for Christmas would have done.

IV

In 1943 Peickert's travels extended to Rumania, to the Peloponnese, to Italy, Denmark, various places in Germany itself, the General Government (formerly Poland), in one particular case even to the Eastern Territories and the Memel. He spent Christmas in the Tyrol. In Italy he got hold of a large quantity of textiles. In Greece he made no purchases, since what was offered was confiscated merchandise; he was afraid that goods which had once been taken away might bring bad luck. Since the spring of 1943 his main source had been trading in gasoline and the Lille-Rumania link for all types of merchandise.

A good man: Army Judge Döhmer

Peickert was suspicious of a friend who was under no obligation to him: Döhmer, army judge of the Sixth Army in the Crimea, later in Rumania. Since Peickert could see no motive for this friendship, he suspected a trap. Kindness was something Döhmer applied to everyone within reach. Like many men trained to associate with vanishing power, Döhmer had the patience to gather men into his net through kindness, on the assumption that they would be of use to him once he had hold of them. So this kindness was really nothing but rapaciousness in another form. Peickert was afraid of Döhmer's kindness. On the other hand he did not want to offend the powerful man. So they were friends.

Fleeting contact with Arlette

After her first visit (two days after they had met at the Café Vaterland) to Peickert's apartment in Berlin, Sächsische Strasse 68, she very soon came again and laid in a small supply of contraceptives. She put them behind some books in the living room, within arm's reach. Peickert never came again to this apartment in the Sächsische Strasse. All plans for meeting Arlette collapsed.

Check zone

Military police were massed in a north-south zone between Fürstenwalde and Schwiebus. Since the fall of 1943 Peickert had preferred to travel close to the front rather than through Germany, barter prospects also becoming more promising closer to the front, i.e., toward the east and southeast.

List of assets

February 1944: 1,000 gallons of sunflower oil in the Olteanu warehouse in Bucharest; a contingent of farm workers on various estates in Podolia; a brothel in Lille with connections to Posen and Kamenez-Podolsk; cash and papers for after the war; valuables in Mannheim, Berlin, Koblenz; two vineyards in the South of France, acquired in exchange for a chance for three French prisoners-of-war (factory managers) to escape; some 45,000 gallons of fuel scattered through various depots in northern Rumania, the Carpathians, Czechoslovakia; a boxcar of lumber en route from the Carpathians to southern Germany; three Rumanian associates; six bales of textiles from Italy; a garden plot in Blankenese, near Hamburg; properties in Posen and Graudenz; supply of eighty travel-warrant blanks; stocks of cigarettes, food concentrates, leathergoods; a partnership in a Leipzig fur business; a concealed

Opel car; complete combat equipment for eight men (including machine pistols and snowshirts).

V

In February 1944 an officer in Lille preferred charges against Peickert for procuring. At the time Peickert was spending his first home leave in the headquarters area of Panzer General Famula, near Targulfrumos, Rumania.

Barter and absolute values

Greater Germany—i.e., the old Reich, occupied, and allied territories—is full of opportunities for barter. Hence there is always, somewhere, a way out, a concealed point, for saving one's life. Like minefields scattered about: absolute values. Values such as: a German soldier is not a procurer, spell death to the transgressor. At this point, barter possibilities cease.

Threat

On February 12, 1944, twenty-four Russian Panzer brigades together with some thirty rifle divisions attacked the Targulfrumos sector of the German front. General Famula's tanks were immobilized due to lack of gasoline.

Relationship to Panzer General Famula

Peickert had never actually spoken to this general. Admiration for this Panzer leader had spread through the staffs of the Sixth and Eighth Armies like a contagion. The general, well known even in peace-time for his bold exploits at horse shows, was in command of the best tanks the German Army had ever had. His general disbelief in a non-victory, supported by the excellent equipment of his troops, rubbed off onto his inferiors. At Targulfrumos his division needed at least 60,000 gallons of gasoline.

Peickert's gasoline stocks within reach of the Famula army

About 3,000 gallons southeast of Jesny, 1,500 gallons west of Ileoai; train with 30,000 gallons of gasoline in the Carpathians. These quantities could be obtained in a day and a half. A further 15,000 gallons could be brought up within two days. These basic stocks could be augmented by a further 10,000 gallons that Peickert was confident he could organize.

Can Peickert afford to act spontaneously?

At first Peickert saw no danger in offering gasoline to Famula. He still did not see his favorite general (whom he thought of as a cross between Tacke and the famous West Prussian equestrian Herr von Westrum) even when he went to inform him that he could supply the necessary quantities of gasoline. The message was taken by an adjutant. The Famula tanks later destroyed a hundred Soviet tanks. As a result the front could be advanced again as far as Jüpan sector.

Famula's maxims

Misgivings always arise. In defiance of them, the only people who achieve success are those capable of deciding to take a leap in the dark. For the future will show greater clemency in judging those who act than those who fail to act.

Famula

Once the terrain and the position have been inspected, the bold decision is usually the best one.

Famula

The experienced supply officer multiplies normal consumption by three.

Famula

Capture

The day after the Panzer victory of Targulfrumos, the second-in-command, Colonel von Posselt, applied for a Knight's Cross for Peickert with the approval of General Famula. Peickert would have preferred a German Cross in gold. A German Cross in gold could have been awarded by any corps commander.

The application for the award of a Knight's Cross to Peickert was received at military personnel headquarters and there led to the arrest of Peickert, who had been charged with living on the avails of prostitution. Peickert was removed to the military prison at Graudenz.

Escape on parole?

Had it been possible to get out of the fortress prison of Graudenz for one day (on parole, for example), Peickert would have been able to reach the Kovno area or the Carpathians. He knew of a partisan hideout there.

General Famula intervenes

The general said to his adjutant: We'll get Peickert out. To Dr. Burdach, a National Socialist official at headquarters, the general said: Peickert lent us a hand, we'll lend Peickert a hand. A lieutenant-colonel who was going to Berlin was instructed to do his utmost for Peickert. The lieutenant-colonel managed to get through by telephone from the Reich capital to the military prison at Graudenz. A few days later a Major von F. was passing through Graudenz. He was a member of the Sixth Army's quartermaster's staff and brought greetings for Peickert. The message was received at the civilian prison in North Graudenz. It was transmitted to the military prison in the fortified zone, but the transmission was delayed, so that the message did not arrive until after sentence had been carried out, i.e., after January 16.

General von Posselt, successor to Famula (who had been transferred to Poland), dictated the following letter, dated November 24, 1944, to the Military Court of Inquiry Prison at Graudenz:

Re: Military prisoner Hans Peickert
Subject: Official request
Ref.: Sentence passed August 3, 1944

I request support for the petition for reprieve on the part of the above-named. During the events at the front over the past year, Peickert has shown endurance, calm, an intelligent grasp, an ability to make decisions and, in particular, personal bravery, and a pardon therefore seems to me worthy of consideration. In view of the extreme shortage of personnel, Peickert is required here.

Date:
Signed:

(General)

Help from von P.?

In response to a postcard he received at the end of 1944 from the Graudenz military prison, von P. sent a telegram via the Foreign Office to the Supreme Command, to be forwarded to the military zone commander in Danzig: Require Sergeant Major Peickert as driver in Ankara. von P.

Last meal
Peickert wanted nothing to eat.

Sentence carried out
On the eve of January 16 Peickert was still confident he would be able to escape. The prison chaplain inquired as to his last wish. Peickert asked for a novel. (Until then he had hardly ever found time to read.) The next morning, while Russian assault troops were approaching Graudenz, Peickert was shot in the yard of the Graudenz fortress by a firing squad. Before he was executed the reasons for the sentence were read out to him.

VI

Posthumous career: Issue No. 234 of the *Infantryman's Bulletin* appeared in July 1962, "Hans Peickert, holder of the Knight's Cross."
Hans F. writes in the Preface:

Whenever the fortunes of war threatened to desert the simple man, events at the front saw the emergence of the action of a single individual whose personality turned the tide. And so it was at Targulfrumos. A whole Panzer division, the one under the command of General Famula, lay immobilized through lack of fuel. And all of a sudden supplies of fuel came rolling in! Hans Peickert, holder of the Knight's Cross, fallen at the front, had obtained the necessary quantities of gasoline from depots behind the lines. The result was a fantastic victory. The front could be advanced as far as the Jüpan sector! May this issue of the Bulletin display the spirit that Hans Peickert, holder of the Knight's Cross, has bequeathed to us as a priceless legacy!

I particularly wish to take this additional opportunity of paying homage to our fallen comrades.

Hans F.

42,000 copies of the pamphlet were printed, of which 41,600 were sold. Further use of the dead Peickert could easily be made with a reissue of the pamphlet after expiry of the eight-month copyright period.

Mandorf

For Theodor W. Adorno on his 60th birthday (11. IX. 1963)

J. G. Fichte, definition of the scholar: In a moral sense the scholar must be the best man of his age.[1] Since June 1932 Mandorf, a political scientist, had renounced his urges and pursued the academic life in the university town of F. He was determined to make an effort.

The academic world

In May 1933 Mandorf, then twenty-three, had to listen to the shameless inaugural address of the incumbent university president H.; since he was sitting within sight of the orating

[1]. Some lectures on the definition of the scholar, 1794, No. 13, p. 261.

president, Mandorf wore an attentive expression.[2] In September he was ordered to take charge of an athletic meet. In 1934 he joined the National Socialist Drivers Corps. In 1935 and 1936 he took part in paramilitary maneuvers.[3] Saturdays and Sundays he worked in his department at the university. On behalf of his Ph.D. counselor he compiled all the footnotes for a publication; he composed indexes for various lecturers. This did little to accelerate his academic career. Nor had it anything to do with the search for truth. As the years passed, Mandorf became an assistant lecturer.[4] A blockage developed in him: he had been waiting too long for his professorship. Many professors regarded a blockage of this kind as necessary for a healthy pursuit of learning. In Mandorf two completely separate desires took shape: he wanted at long last to become a professor; on the other hand he desired a more comprehensive, purer dedication, "since all learning," as Schelling says, "is one and the same thing, and every variation of it is merely a link in the organism of the whole: since all the sciences and every branch

2. After a while he became attentive, simply because he wore an attentive expression.

3. Howitzer practice, fast marches, mathematical tests, forced marches; at the end of the maneuvers, a march-past, with equipment, in front of the commanding general, who saluted with drawn sword.

4. Salary Class A-13, with subsequent eligibility for a pension. One reason for Mandorf's slow advancement was that his special field (structural phases in the woven textile industry, in particular cupro-acetate rayon) did not at that time appear to be capable of much development. When Mandorf began, it was still a potentially interesting problem. Mandorf, whose father was a civil servant and whose paternal grandfather a farmer, did not have the knack of quickly laying aside subjects once he had taken them up. Professor Eu. said he had embarked on his subject too seriously.

of learning are parts of a philosophy, that is, of the striving to participate in primordial knowledge." [5]

Mandorf's radius of action

Mandorf's impotent ideas had been populating a number of publications since 1934. Their dissemination was limited to technical journals.[6] With a wider dissemination his ideas would have brought about their own suppression, since they were incompatible with the existing order; since 1934 Mandorf had been waiting for the awakening of the nation to alter the national economy as well; but the awakening did not affect it. Mandorf's choice, therefore, was between impotence of his ideas due to too little publicity and impotence of these ideas due to more publicity, which could not have been tolerated. Mandorf worked steadily toward his goal. In 1939 he obtained his Ph.D. He was about to give his inaugural lecture when war broke out.

Satisfying his urges

The first teacher whom Mandorf encountered enticed him to become a good student. Through a system of reward and punishment, the school he attended after primary school prompted him to become interested in Latin and mathematics. The advantages associated with excellent reports were too attractive to be renounced: so Mandorf studied political science. In addition to this, Professor W. infected Mandorf with some

---

5.   Second lecture on the method of academic study, Jena 1802, conclusion.

6.   *Financial Record,* 1936, pp. 212–214; *Political Science Review,* vol. 2, pp. 430 ff.; 1938, pp. 1044 ff.; *Business World,* 1937, pp. 12 ff.; *Credit and Soil,* 1938, pp. 114 ff. (review); *Bemberg Rayon,* special issue 1938; *Wool and Industry,* 1938, pp. 425 ff.; 1939, pp. 4320 ff.

of Plato's ideas.[7] Since Mandorf was devoting his intelligence to the search for truth, he could not at the same time use it to attend to his interests.[8] No girl ever wanted to visit his

7. W. was a very lean man. When he talked about Plato he leaned against his desk in an attitude indicating indifference to the body. This attitude betokened physical frailty (to the advantage of intellectual activity). Seen over a period of several decades W. demonstrated great physical toughness. The energy he saved by being conservative he invested in toughness. This toughness was useful to his thinking apparatus. His thinking apparatus was useful to his livelihood as a professor in F. In this way W.'s body was well looked after all round.

8. On May 26, 1933, the sixty-eight professors of F. University who were searching for the truth gathered in the second university quadrangle for a ceremony:

1st batch: (12th to 17th centuries)

Twenty-four members of the higher faculties with purple caps, senior jurists, members of the medical faculty, aristocrats, fourteen theologians.

2nd batch: (18th to 19th centuries)

Scientists, whose fields were narrow, specialized subjects, with a quite different background, of course, from their colleagues; since the early nineteenth century the scientific institutes lay scattered about the town of F. as if by an explosion. The scientists wore caps with red stripes. What they would have liked to do best was dissect live ducks. That was partially forbidden. Some members of the medical faculty belonged *ipso facto* to this batch, others did not. One assistant woman doctor kept her prematurely born fetus in a refrigerator belonging to the institute. Professor B., the pathologists' pope, pointed out to her that this was not very humane behavior.

3rd batch: (early 19th century)

Twelve philologists, seven philosophers, two legal historians, two medical historians, four historians, one orientalist, one archeologist, one palimpsest expert with yellow stripes on his gown.

New batch: mostly younger men, physical education instruc-

wretched apartment. His interest in such adventures petered out. And yet Mandorf achieved neither a professorship nor the truth. Going for walks along narrow woodland paths in the environs of F. did not satisfy him. Thus the only urge that Man-

---

tors, musicologists, fencing instructors, assistant lecturers.

4th batch: (from 1910)

Political scientists, not yet occupying an undisputed place in the hierarchy of the sciences; hence their special efforts to adhere to scientific methods. Likewise wearing sixteenth-century gowns.

The head of the Philosophy Department, who as President of the University represented the academic world, addressed those assembled in the quadrangle:

Albert Leo Schlageter, he said, had died the bitterest and the sublimest of deaths. Not in the front line as leader of an infantry battery, but facing French rifles, defenseless; yet stand he did, and he endured the worst! Even this would have been bearable in a final shout of triumph, had a victory been fought for and won. Instead, darkness, humiliation and betrayal. Thus at his bitterest moment he had had to commit his most *sublime* act. Whence came the iron resolve enabling him to withstand the worst? Whence came the purity of heart enabling him to confront his soul with the sublimest and the highest? Student of F.! Know and remember when you tread the hero's native soil, driving or walking in the mountains, the forest, or the valleys, that primeval rock and granite have been helping through the ages to create that iron resolve. Defenseless, the hero's inner eye had turned away from the muzzles of the rifles he was facing, toward the mountains of his native land. Albert Leo Schlageter met his death, the bitterest and the sublimest, with an iron resolve and a pure heart.

The ceremony ended with singing. Needless to say, no one did any research during these stirring days. The following day the political scientists and the members of the medical faculty had faculty meetings. The jurists were busy with state examinations. The theologians were working on a resolution, the philologists on a change in the statutes.

dorf could still follow was a warped urge toward learning, one which had taken root in him at the time when he was first enticed to devote himself to learning: the ever-renewed urge to entice others to devote themselves to learning.[9]

Misfortune as a habit

In 1938 Mandorf was supposed to become head lecturer; the plan was dropped. The office would have entailed limited power. Those who find themselves in a position of power can think, because they are participating in reality. But the exercise of power leaves very little opportunity for thought. The scholar, however, has this opportunity to a high degree.[10] Mandorf had become accustomed to his inadequately heated study. Nowhere in this provincial town could you get a good cup of coffee; Mandorf might have been shocked by a good cup of coffee. He regarded the meager financial resources of a lecturer-in-the-making as palladium of his vocation; the position retained something of the ancient freedom of the private scholar. The lack of records, books, and aids at his department was also regarded by Mandorf as being part of that freedom: it enabled the mind to move on a plane above earthly things.[11]

For a while, in the spring of 1937, Mandorf pursued a

9. In Mandorf's ears the words: If you can sense the impending suffering of the world and mankind, if you can willingly make the sacrifice of renouncing it, if you believe you possess the strength to do this, then become a teacher.

10. Mandorf's only contact with power was through Dr. von L. in the Army.

11. Professor G. used to say: Take Schopenhauer for example, he never received a professorship, yet think of all he wrote! Remember the case of Dr. C. This colleague was made head of a department; as soon as he joined a department he ceased to work. Productive energy and financial resources should be kept severely apart!

young woman. She nearly forced a joint vacation on him. After escaping from this predicament Mandorf was very content with his solitary existence. The material from which Mandorf composed his duty was ambition on the one hand, his livelihood on the other: he was spurred on by what he did not get; had he got more, there might have been nothing left to spur him on. One of the junior staff who was a close friend of Mandorf's was expelled from the university. In the fall of 1938 Mandorf broke his ankle on the worn cobblestones of F. The subject of political science did not permit excursions into ancient texts, which Mandorf would have liked to undertake. Always the same menu at the restaurant where he ate every day; he did not dare change restaurants because his associates might talk and assume he had quarreled with the proprietress. Extreme mental effort, earnest efforts to compensate by sport.[12] It was not that Mandorf was unaware of his misfortune; but at the same time misfortune blocked most avenues of escape from his unfortunate plight.

Last stand, 1939

In his desperate state Mandorf yearned for change. Trained by seven years in the service of science and learning, Mandorf was now ready, when the war broke out, to let his personality unfold.

12. But Mandorf never wore casual clothes. As a matter of principle he wore expensive business suits of English woolens, and his shirts were always carefully chosen. On February 16, 1346, Count Rheinstein did not wear chainmail while traveling from Heudeber to Danstedt. The village youths killed him because they did not realize he belonged to a higher class. Mandorf, who belonged to a minority, felt a similar need to protect himself (wearing a business suit was like appearing in armor). He had to be well dressed if he wanted to escape being exterminated by mistake!

> *To transform as much of the world as possible, yes, the whole world, into oneself, means Life in the highest sense of the word.*
> Wilhelm von Humboldt
> *Letter to Caroline*

As soon as war broke out, things started moving. In the winter of 1939 Mandorf married Countess N., a student at F. (the family came originally from Bavaria; since 1922 many members had been living in Bucharest). His associates in F. were dubious about this sudden marriage. N. was among the students entrusted to Mandorf in his capacity of lecturer, so in that sense she could be considered a "dependent." The wedding took place in the village of W. The fear that actually never left him when he was with a woman seemed negligible to Mandorf.[13] Next he was called up for special duties in the Army being formed for the campaign in France; then followed a journey together to Bucharest made possible despite wartime visa difficulties. Mandorf and his new wife spent three to five hours over lunch; in contrast to these meals was the former hasty gulping down of food which had meant no more than an interruption of his freedom. Early in 1940 a new work by Mandorf was published. Mandorf's participation in the Western campaign consisted of being sent in June 1940 for a few days to Bordeaux, where he was put in charge of some textile factories. With an increasing sense of reality Mandorf began to examine his interests. He was sure of his wife. In the hills surrounding F. she tried to buy a villa for their conjugal residence. His nights of lovemaking with his wife were spent in the hope that they would make his personality unfold; when

13. By marrying her Mandorf forestalled a colleague who was trying to have him called before a court of inquiry in an affair of honor.

this activity failed to enrich him, he reduced it. His wife thought he was going through a change of mood.

Army Headquarters in Rumania summoned Mandorf. On April 8, 1941, he crossed into Greece; on April 9 he entered Salonica. To Greece, Germany, Italy, England, in other words, to those involved, this campaign was a nuisance. The front advanced southward according to plan. April 12 brought skirmishes in the Klidi Pass and at Lake Kastoria, by April 14 the roads approaching Mount Olympus were already congested. None of the Greeks wanted to go on fighting. As a member of the century's victorious party, Mandorf felt a kind of physical pleasure in victory and rapid movement. He was regarded as an expert on textile factories and the Greek language. Following a Panzer staff as far as Corinth, Mandorf wore his hair extremely short at the sides that year. The hair on top of his head—kept short for combat purposes—was neatly parted. When he saw his wife again, after she had come as far as Zagreb to meet him, he did not recognize her. The limbs that a year ago had ensnared him now seemed scarcely worth looking at. He had penetrated deeper into reality, he had already left last year's condition behind. The train by which N. wanted to leave Zagreb was hopelessly overcrowded. His pistol enabled Mandorf to find a seat for N. in the stifling throng.

In June 1941 Mandorf was flown to Crete on account of his linguistic abilities. He could still see some of Crete's conquerors at Maleme airport, waiting to be flown out. On Crete Mandorf had a staff of two interpreters. He divided the map of Crete up into squares.[14] Headquarters were far away in

14. Crete consists mostly of rocky mountains. Here and there olives grow, and in the western part of the island oranges. In the

Athens. On Crete Mandorf got along fairly well with the first adjutant of the fortress commandant, a Major von R.[15] But his relations with German friends were already cooling off. His mood of victory became a kind of plunging into the foreign country, a shedding of his skin by which he once and for all cast off his past—or, as he could already say: his pasts. He sought contact with some of the rich families in Heraklion.

---

gorges of the eastern part there are almond trees. Goats and torrents prevent growth on the island.

Crete lay there conquered. The proportion of those killed was one German to every ten Englishmen; from that aspect there was no doubt as to the victory.

15. In the fall of 1942 the — Infantry Division to which von R. had belonged since the Sudeten crisis, went to Crete. At the beginning of 1942 this division had the highest losses of the whole Army. The division had bad luck. First it was used for the air landing in Holland. Thirty loaded machines were shot down by the enemy. Machines that landed on the airstrips caught fire and burned. The division was then transferred to Salzwedel. At an artillery demonstration there, a shell landed among the spectators. The crossing of the Dnestr in southern Russia took place with heavy losses. The figures of captured equipment now began to increase. Lieutenant Grave died uttering the words: "Mission accomplished!" Lieutenant Taddigen died shouting: "Long live the 7th Company!" The division was transferred to Crete. It continued to improve on Crete. The staff headquarters were hidden in the interior of the island. The plan was to conduct the island's defense by means of attack. This was how the British found the division when they removed it from Crete in June 1945.

Ambitious Major von R., who was adept at handling people, consulted Mandorf in a variety of personal matters; while the officer did not follow his advice, the result was that Mandorf let his behavior on Crete be governed by consideration for von R. He saw too late that these confidential talks were part of the leadership methods that von R. sometimes applied even unconsciously.

Scarcely had Mandorf finally divested himself of his past, or his changing pasts, on Crete and his personality had unfolded for the second time during the war, when his original past took possession of him again; he tried to entice his Greek friends to devote themselves to learning. Mandorf's sense of totality was applied to the whole population of Crete that was in need of education. At the same time, his individually slanted pedagogic Eros was directed at the eighteen powerful families of the country. Who will respond most quickly to an appeal to the intellectual side of man? The one who wishes to disguise material interests with intellectual activity. Evening classes started by Mandorf in Heraklion for urban children did not prosper.[16] Mandorf gave lectures on German language and literature, in particular Novalis. His new-found friends were very surprised to find that Novalis' real name was something quite different. Mandorf won over the Natr. and Kar. families. At the home of the Metropoulos family he met the sixteen-year-old boy G.; this new penetration of reality caused an upheaval in the scholar, holding him captive for a considerable time.[17]

16. In the towns on Crete there were a sprinkling of independent Jews, artisans, the odd professor or two, a number of Greek Orthodox priests. The mountainous regions, where there were no villages, were inhabited by shepherds and casual laborers. In effect the essential part of the population was grouped around the eighteen or so families who controlled the island. There were misgivings about undermining the organically developed authority by providing this clientele with excessive education.

Over Mandorf's protests Major von R. cut off financial support for the evening classes after the beginnings had shown no success. Mandorf asked the Ferania family for help. The Feranias were stingy.

17. During an air raid the retarded, fragile G. Metropoulos found himself without the keeper who usually accompanied him. Mandorf

Through the Metropoulos family he met the Si.'s and the large Fer. family, who at once procured the support of the W. and Be. families for the forces of occupation, these families being more or less in control of the eastern part of the island. The families were trying to trade with the mainland. For this it was essential to be on good terms with the German forces of occupation. Mandorf actually had something quite different in mind.

Learning's position as a servant
Amor scientie factus exulis. The lover of learning is banished from power. So he must serve power. In former times the learned men were among the better-paid servants of the aristocracy. Today they serve learning as civil servants. The fact that Mandorf could not use the instrument of learning for his own purposes was due to its having been created from the very beginning as a servant. Abelard, Bruno, Petrarch, Goethe, Humboldt, served their masters. When Abelard and Bruno no longer wished to serve, they were eliminated.

Description of Mandorf
Weak, liberal (easily misled)
Outsider
Reconciler of peoples
Unifier
He wore his hair longer now, there was no fat on his body, Mandorf was not reconciled to his situation.

In 1943/44 he could have changed his identity, discarded

---

came across him in the storerooms. Mandorf was bewildered to find that the feeble-minded youth clung to him. Mandorf first took this for love: the exceptional danger, the lack of a keeper, desire. Naturally this did not last long.

As a family the Metropoulos's were swarthy, stocky, rather large-boned.

his nationality. One of the Greek partisan bands that was supported by the property-owning families as a defense against other bands suggested this to him.[18]

Taming of an eluder

N., whom he had almost forgotten, got in touch with him from Salonica. Mandorf flew there that same night. He managed to bring the intractable woman under control again.[19]

In August 1944 Russian units were threatening the upper Balkans from the northeast. Even in this situation the German command did not want to abandon Greece. It decided on a partial evacuation of Crete. The soldiers who remained behind withdrew to what was known as the inner fortress of Crete. Greek partisans coming down from the Ida Mountains moved into the area deserted by the Germans. Their advisers were British officers. During the evacuation of Heraklion, Mandorf saw through the telescope one of these officers directing the traffic of the partisans entering the city. During the days following the German troops' evacuation of the eastern part of the island, the British liaison officers lost control over the partisans. Mandorf heard that members of the families he had won over to the cause of learning were being shot. He requested General B., the commander of the fortress, to send a relief ex-

18. Panduvas, the partisan leader, would have liked to have Mandorf for his chief of staff. Mandorf did not take up the suggestion out of consideration for his friend Major von R. Von R. was well informed about the events of July 20, 1944, in Germany. He discussed with Mandorf the possibility of organizing an anti-Hi. resistance movement on Crete.

19. Mandorf could never hear Mozart's horn concerto without thinking of that first hesitating embrace of N. (still exhilarated by the stirring first of May holiday).

pedition to save his friends.[20] His request was refused. Mandorf tried to get through to Heraklion himself. But Mandorf had emerged from the tranquillity of learning in order to make a woman happy; he had given her up to celebrate victories; he had dissociated himself from the victors to slip into a Cretan skin, all this to unfold his personality on which forty threatened people were now depending; now he would have liked to resume his original activity; he would have liked to observe the rapidly deteriorating situation as a scholar. For a time he analyzed which was more important: to sacrifice himself for his friends or not to sacrifice himself and set up a memorial to them by a portrait, i.e., by means of a book he planned to write after the war.

20. On that 24th of August, the iron men sang all day long over Radio Agram. Mandorf heard:

Why don't you want me?
One day the sky will be blue again.
I don't want
That's for sure!
After yesterday comes a tomorrow.
Try
D'you see the chow dog in the garden?
Why?
There'll always be love.
Down there in the partisan village the wind is blowing.
The bells ring out to the starry sky.
Down there in the ocean lies the past.
And dreams are of loveliness.
I need no castle.
I need today and for all eternity.
Be kinder.

The Kaulos family had always been cautious; they had never offered their hospitality to Mandorf or associated in any other way with the forces of occupation. Nevertheless they were now hanged with all the rest.

Concept of personality

General B. forbade Mandorf to try any more sorties.[21] Mandorf the scholar had thought out a system on Crete. But even if his practical training had been better, the house of cards would have collapsed: it was supported by Mandorf's person. This was supported by events. Event themselves were not supported. Thus Mandorf was not supported.

Mandorf the expert

Actually Mandorf was not an expert in anything.

An appalling discovery

During the disastrous days of Heraklion, Mandorf made a discovery: he was indifferent to everything that had happened or was happening. As a matter of fact he was even indifferent to this moral breakdown. But his indifference to the misfortunes of his friends deprived Mandorf's whole campaign of its meaning. Mandorf's personality lay there unfolded: it contained nothing.[22]

21. Sacrifices: Not to go into the garden, but study Latin instead. Not to drink, but get up early instead. If Mandorf sacrificed what he did not want he was bound to arrive at what he did want. Were personality assets being lost in this sacrifice of Mandorf's real intention (to help his friends)? It was necessary to choose: potential assets, or maneuverability with a view to higher tasks.

22. Mandorf was active and fully occupied these days. He wrote telegrams to Salonica. Every day until one o'clock he did his usual map-plotting duties, he went through the reports coming in from Chania and Rethymnon; he was the only man with the rank of sergeant who understood the language of the country. He grimly continued submitting his requests in writing to General B. He would have missed the conflict if B. had suddenly given in and sent an expedition to Heraklion.

General B. had had enough. He did not like the look in Mandorf's eyes. In September he sent him with a night flight via Kos to Agram. A military headquarters there had a job for Mandorf. He was ordered to investigate the traffic situation on the Larina-Ziotyon-Trinkalla highway as far as Olympus. The road was congested, as in 1941. Mandorf was still—at the end of 1944—regarded as an expert by the members of a corps staff. One evening he was allowed to recite from Plato's *Apologia*.[23] At that time the corps staff to which Mandorf was attached received an offer from the anti-Communist resistance group EDES to take out Greek nationality. The idea was to proceed jointly against the Communists. The members of the corps staff, afraid of their legal status as future prisoners-of-war, declined. Mandorf, spiritually exhausted, fought until June 1945 on the side of EDES against Communists. He fell into Yugoslav hands. As soon as he got his breath back he used

---

23. Gentlemen, said the commanding general, this evening we have the pleasure of welcoming Professor Mandorf among us. Mr. Mandorf has consented to recite some passages from his own translation. After these trying days a pause for mental refreshment of this kind seems to me both desirable and appropriate. I request your attention. With these words the evening was opened. Dinner was followed by the recitation and a social hour: classical records were played. The overall atmosphere was subdued, there being some doubt as to whether or not enemy units had occupied a pass near Franquilla.

As an encore Mandorf recited "The Pretorians," by Victor Hugo:

We were ten,
We took the town
And captured the King himself!
Afterward,
Masters of the town and the port,
We knew not what more to do,
And so we courteously
Gave back the town to the King.

it to learn the International; Mandorf stayed until 1946. Back in Germany he found none of his friends. His wife discovered his hiding place,[24] asked him to agree to a divorce; this took place in 1952. Mandorf had no claims to be reinstated. For a full professorship he lacked his 1939 inaugural lecture.[25] Even if he had achieved full professorship, he would not have been given a department because no department head knew him and Mandorf did not push himself forward. In 1958 he was given a post as assistant lecturer. In 1959 he advanced to the post of tutor. He has a good chance of one day being offered a permanent place on the faculty council.[26] In 1960 he married his housekeeper. Should he have one more encounter with reality, it would find him prepared, although somewhat worn out.

24. In 1948 Mandorf took on a job as a private tutor in Butzbach, Hesse. He did not show his face in the towns in which he used to live. Nevertheless with the aid of a returning prisoners' organization his wife discovered his whereabouts.

25. A professor who knew Mandorf slightly and who himself had been unfairly treated took up Mandorf's case. Thereupon a file lay for some time before the Board of Governors of the University of F. and was studied. At the Ministry, Department IV (University Department) passed the file on to Department I (Legal, Organization, Budget). This department sought to arrive at an interpretation that would have been favorable to Mandorf. But the Finance Ministry's expert raised objections to it. The file was then handed back with no decision to the University Board of Governors. Although the professor who was slightly acquainted with Mandorf wielded considerable influence at the time, he did not concern himself any further with the file; his helpfulness was without any ulterior motive, it sufficed for single actions.

26. This would depend on the gradual implementation of the recommendations of the faculty council at the University of M. The President and the Board of Governors have indicated that they are basically in favor of these recommendations. In conjunction with the local government, steps have been initiated. On the other hand, these steps must not infringe upon the traditional ideas of the academic world as laid down in the university constitution.

Lieutenant Boulanger

I

In February 1942 the head of the Department of Anatomy at the Reich University of Strassburg, Professor A. Hirt, sent the following communication to one of the leading men in the Reich Government:

Re: Securing of craniums of Jewish-Bolshevist commissars for purposes of scientific investigation at the Reich University of Strassburg

Cranium collections are on hand representing almost every race and people. The Jews are the only group for which science has an insufficient number of craniums at its disposal for the obtaining of conclusive results. The war in Eastern Europe now provides an opportunity of remedying this deficiency. Jewish-Bolshevist commissars, the embodiment of a repulsive but typical subhuman species, make it possible for us to lay hands on tangible scientific proof by securing their craniums.

The most efficient method of acquiring and preserving this cranium material is in the form of instructions to the Army henceforth to immediately hand over all Jewish-Bolshevist commissars alive to the military police. The military police will in turn receive special instructions to report to a specified location the number and whereabouts of these prisoners as they are delivered and to see that they are kept under close guard pending the arrival of a specially authorized officer. The officer charged with the securing of this material (a junior medical officer, or a medical student, attached to the Army or possibly the military police, and supplied with car and driver) will take a prearranged series of photographs and anthropological measurements and to the best of his ability will establish origin, date of birth, and other personal data. When the death of the Jew has subsequently been brought about, in a way which will not damage the head, the officer will separate the head from the trunk and, after immersing it in preserving fluid in a metal container (with a close-fitting lid) specially provided for the purpose, will forward it to its destination. The photographs, measurements, and other data pertinent to the head and eventually to the skull will permit the laboratory to embark on comparative anatomical research, as well as study of the racial origin, pathological features of the cranium formation, brain formation and size, and many additional aspects.

By virtue of its functions and objectives the new Reich University of Strassburg would appear to be the most suitable place for the preservation and study of the cranium material thus acquired.

A. Hirt

The Personnel Department of the Army offered Lieutenant Rudolf B., of Flörsheim (on the Main), the command of this special mission. Boulanger had been a medical student. In effect, the acceptance of this special mission meant a short cut to promotion. The prospect of a transfer to research was held out. Boulanger seized the opportunity.

II

In 1942 Rudolf B. was thirty-four years old. He was of medium height. His complexion was olive, his eyelids were hairless. He may have had Romans or (eighteenth-century) Frenchmen among his ancestors. He had volunteered for the engineering corps, was prepared to shine, to seize advantages, to arrive at speedy solutions. For years he found no opportunity of conquering, he did not pass his state medical examination, he had no technical qualifications. All he had were good intentions, and with this he waited for his chance, which came in 1942.

Good intentions

If executing a task consists of proceeding straight ahead along a prescribed path without flagging or allowing oneself to be impeded, it might be said that B. fulfilled such a task in the highest degree. Vigor and intelligence operated—if, like Seneca, one is to regard a human being as a marching army—in this case on the very center of the front. In practice, however, none of B.'s activities proceeded along a straightforward course. Problems of ambiguity arose, and his determination to succeed was not enough to solve these. In cases of this kind there is no such thing as good intentions since good intentions are beside the point. B. decided such ambiguous cases on the basis of the greatest effectiveness.

What he would actually rather have been

Since boyhood B. had wanted to be a hydraulic engineer. However, there was no school of hydraulic engineering near Flörsheim (on the Main). After his graduation, therefore, Boulanger decided to study medicine in Frankfurt (on the Main). Difficulty in passing the state examination put an end to his studies. B. was drafted into the Army.

Advantages of his new post

On taking over his special mission Boulanger became eligible for a front-line allowance of Reichsmark 2.65 per day. Lieutenant Boulanger was responsible for the allotting of duties, more particularly hours of duty. Later on he sometimes took advantage of this in order to make a brief excursion to some place of interest in Russia. Furthermore, there was the possibility of being invited to various staff headquarters where one could make lifelong friendships. Thirdly, there was the chance of procuring extra blankets, supplies, and rations at various commissariats, a relatively easy matter for a mobile outfit such as B.'s special detachment. Finally there was no overlooking the fact that the connection with the academic world, even if only as an agent, had advantages of a prestige nature.

Superiority of the academic world

A connection with the academic world means lifelong security. The academic world is free. The members of the academic world rank immediately behind Party members, at social functions they come after the S.S. but before the German East Africans.

Chain of command

In disciplinary matters B. in his new post came under the command of the Army Personnel Department as represented by the Army Group chiefs, who were in turn represented by the senior Army Corps general commanding the odd-numbered Army Corps. B. had no dealings with any of the senior Army judges. In fact the only superior who could give him orders was the academic world. In a formal sense B. also came under the jurisdiction of the divisional commander of whatever sector of the front he happened to be in. If necessary B. could absent himself from their jurisdiction by moving to a different divisional area. But no conflicts arose.

Relationship to an officer's honor

At times during the years following 1942 B. found his butcher's duties—which other officers compared to a hangman's job—abhorrent. Some officers entrusted with this task might have taken to drink. While working on his very first case B. had to overcome mental inhibitions. In this particular instance B. deserted his post just as the head was being severed, thus incurring the risk of his assistants making mistakes. B.'s thought: You must not take to drink now.

On the other hand, there are no genuine inhibitions involved in killing someone else if one can see clearly enough that it is not one's own death that is taking place. B.'s sense of insecurity during much of the procedure was based mainly on the disapproval of his activities by various officers with whom he was friendly. But this disapproval was not valid. When B. later rejected one or another of the commissars delivered to him by the Army, these same officers, who criticized his special mission, were in command of the firing squad executing the commissar (which usually resulted in mutilating the head).

Relations with women
Excellent.

Prison life

For many men the conquest of Eastern Europe meant a removal of barriers after years of conforming to a narrow way of life. Hence the occupation of the East should by rights have brought with it rape and pillage, or at least an adequate number of brothels. Instead, the occupation was carried out according to regulations which might just as well have been those of a prison administration. In this respect the great liberation of Eastern Europe in 1941 and the following years coincided for B. with the greatest disappointment of his life.

Initial visit to Professor Hirt

Luncheon at Professor Hirt's consisted of four courses: chicken bisque, fish, saddle of venison, macédoine of fruits. The professor's nieces had been invited for coffee. It was late afternoon by the time Boulanger took leave. He could almost have fallen in love with one of the nieces. Next morning he boarded his eastbound train.

Activities started in the region of Orel. Not everyone handed over to Boulanger was a commissar. It turned out that the number of commissars was being exaggerated and the classifying of commissars as "Jewish-Bolshevist" was arbitrary. Most of them were simply partisan leaders who had been arbitrarily classified as commissars. While the Army showed great reluctance to deliver officers taken prisoner at the front, it was most liberal in handing over partisans, although experience showed that commissars were more likely to be found among the officers. However, the Army officers did take back partisans when required (and then shot them themselves), exchanging them for captured front commissars whom they handed over to the military police.

The main problem consisted of the proper classification of

the prisoners as commissars and of the use of the additional criterion "Jewish-Bolshevist." Not every Jewish-Russian officer came into this category, nor did every Bolshevik. Boulanger tried to obtain data on the question: with what rank in the Party hierarchy does an officer become a commissar? From several staff officers whom he questioned he received inconclusive data that only served to convince him even further of the arbitrariness of the selection methods. The care which he devoted to the execution of his special mission, and the extra research that went into the clarifying of its basic principles, was on a par with the care which otherwise in the Army would have only been expended on the awarding of the highest decorations. At some headquarters this earned B.'s unit the title of "Decorations Detachment." Even a negatively evaluated mission—in fact, especially such a mission—must be accomplished with all the energy and intelligence at one's command. In so doing, one must compensate for what has not been thoroughly thought out or is subject to criticism in the original definition of one's duties. Despite his efforts Boulanger knew he could not avoid making any number of errors, and that these were sometimes to the prisoners' advantage and sometimes to their disadvantage. The errors in favor of Russians (e.g., those who were not classified as Jews although they were Jews) could be compensated for by safety margins, a procedure which was not permissible in the case of the erroneous inclusion of innocent persons (e.g., Jews who were not commissars, commissars who were not Jews), since in such cases a safety margin, while it reduced the probability of error, at the same time jeopardized the effectiveness of the method. In actual practice the only way to determine racial origin was by such primitive factors as appearance, family and first names, or perhaps skull measurements. The strong possibility of error made it seem advisable to discontinue the mission altogether. By the same token it followed that, if the mission were continued, the errors must be tolerated and allowed for in the calculations. So Boulanger was beset by endless doubts, but he felt that these doubts must not be permitted to hamper the careful and conscientious execution of his mission. It was therefore important to him to convey his ideas and good intentions to an area where they could not harm the performance of his duties: during this period he read philosophical works, as he was toying with the idea of later extending his (previously abandoned) studies to this subject.

III

The task of bringing precision into the hopeless end of the captured commissars completely occupied B. during the summer and winter of 1942 in the areas of the Central and Southern Army Groups (later of the two Southern Army Groups). In February 1943 his sphere of activity was limited to the Central Army Group. At that time Boulanger no longer restricted himself to a superficial anthropological examination and to obtaining of personal data before having the prisoners killed; he now had informal talks with the commissars in order to retain an impression not only of their external appearance but of their minds. The body of thought thus committed to paper immediately before the writers' death served, B. believed, as additional research material; this sense of quality enhanced B.'s respect for the mission entrusted to him. It is probably always true that to a certain extent one identifies oneself with the enemy one kills (prior thereto one has just seen him alive). Thus Boulanger identified himself, as it were, with the intellectual achievements of his object of study. He did not know what his attitude should be when he was conscious of such feelings. Perhaps B. could, while conforming to his orders, have adapted his method to his feelings at the time by continually extending the respite accorded the prisoners to make their written statements; but since his feelings had not the degree of clarity evinced by his former methods, he kept to his former methods.

In the summer of 1943 a further difficulty arose, the problem of increasing numbers. First the Central Army Group retreated from the Orel bulge. The prisoner-of-war camps situated behind the front had to be hurriedly evacuated. This in turn necessitated an accelerated screening in these camps on the part of Boulanger's detachment. At times the decision as to whether or not a case in point was a Jewish-Bolshevist commissar had to be delegated. This meant that the depots sometimes received heads and descriptions where obvious mistakes had been made. Any change in the procedure would presumably have increased this confusion.

During the late summer of 1943 the Russians took advantage of the gap forming between the southern and central German fronts (a gap which the High Command was bending every effort to close) by attacking at an entirely different point. On the day of the offensive a crisis developed in the Second Army. The base units and the prisoner-of-war camps were caught up in the retreat. The 33rd Panzer Division brought up as a reinforcement found itself involved in the offensive while it was still aboard the trains. Desperate staffs tried to stem the retreat by maintaining their old headquarters. During these days Boulanger's detachment, which was taking along six Russian officers, found itself near the junction of Schlichta, not far from Smolensk. Close to a wooded area Boulanger's assistants were attacked by partisans. Boulanger himself was wounded and escaped with the vehicles in the van of the convoy. It was later assumed by the Russians that the leader of the "Decorations Detachment" was among those captured by the partisans.

The experience was a shock to Boulanger. Surrounded by victorious German troops, by staffs which raised no objections, and in the service of scientific research, there is no sense of guilt; suddenly the situation changes: like a draft springing up, a sense of guilt arises from which one must protect oneself, just as in early spring one has to be careful of open doors, for these only bring colds or even pneumonia.

IV

Boulanger spent the last days of 1943 and part of 1944 at the Wiesbaden Area Military Hospital. The collapse of the Central Army Group in August 1944 dashed B.'s hopes of promotion. A transfer to research was also out of the question. A transfer to civilian research, which would have been possible on Professor A. Hirt's recommendation, was not feasible because of B.'s complete recovery. Military research at that particular time was concentrating on special problems to which Boulanger's Eastern European experience had nothing to contribute. Instead he was transferred after his recovery to the "Central Administration of Austrian Prisoner-of-War Camps."

One more opportunity for total dedication presented itself to Boulanger before the end of the war, in Vienna. In January 1945 the doomed city, like a shrine, attracted troops and officers within its walls—if one can speak here of walls to be defended rather than, perhaps more properly, palaces, canals, and hills. On January 14 General Rendulic took over the defense of the city and had a thousand soldiers strung up. On January 18 (twenty-four hours later an air raid destroyed the opera house) the young Party Area Chief's augmented staff, which included Boulanger, attended a performance of *Lohengrin*. The night of January 21/22, after two days of quiet, the Russians embarked on a new major assault on Vienna. Within a few hours the opportunity of meeting death here was exhausted. Russian panzers were lined up on the northern bank of the canal; practically speaking the city was in Russian hands. All that remained of the last great chance was the biological factor pure and simple. B. managed to reach the American lines. There he gave himself up.

V

How do people like B. live today?

In the summer of 1961 reporters tracked Boulanger down as a packer in a paper mill near Cologne. His offenses were subject to statutory limitations. A correspondent from *L'Humanité* asked for an interview. B. was ushered into the board room and answered questions. When asked about his present beliefs he replied that he was a Marxist. What was he doing? There was nothing one could do.

Contagion from the enemy

He said he had been infected, as it were, by his enemies, since naturally he had talked to some of the prisoners. Did that mean he thought the imperialists in the German Federal Republic were in particular danger of becoming Communists? Of course not. One would have to be in closer contact with the enemy. Chop off his head? In a sense, yes. That was carrying the Christian spirit too far, said the reporter from *L'Humanité*.

Renewed encounter with the academic world

The war over, there was a chance of resuming his studies as soon as the universities reopened. He was given credit for four prewar semesters.

Expiation and surrogate

Question: I see by your forehead that you joined a students' dueling club?

Answer: That was another compromise.

Question: But how did you land in jail?

Answer: After a row with the principal of the Institute at Marburg in 1953, I tried to start up in business on my own, in the textile branch. This fresh start ended in disaster, that's to say I had trouble making payments and so they put me in jail.

Question: With criminals?

Answer: They don't make any distinction.

Question: How many years?

Answer: Three. The prison padre regarded it as an expiation for my deeds during the war.

Question: You mean he forgave you because they were commissars?

Answer: In his eyes the prison sentence made everything all right. He thought I might go and look after lepers in Ethiopia.

Question: What kind of a job would that be?

Answer: You get leprosy too, but in return you can save the lives of a few lepers.

Question: Not a very fair deal, to exchange some sixty to a hundred well-trained key men for five or six lepers saved in Ethiopia. For that you would have to believe that all men are equal.

Answer: I agree absolutely. Of course it's not a sensible exchange.

Question: Then, if I understand you correctly, you are now carrying on the existences of the men you murdered?

Answer: No.

Question: What are you doing in a positive sense?

Answer: I've already told you: one's not allowed to do anything. Just have a conviction.

Question: That's something!

Answer: But the change in me is not meant either as expiation or surrogate.

How the "decorations" method worked

We usually arrived in the evening, because in the morning we were busy somewhere else with dissecting, embalming, etc., and sometimes we covered considerable distances during the day—our day began at 5 A.M. and was never over before midnight; toward evening we would reach a depot, arriving in our jeeps with trailers carrying the instruments and other material. Sometimes there were headquarters near by, and we would be invited for a bite to eat or a drink, but often they would ignore us, especially during our first visit to the boundary-sector divisions of the Northern Army Group, which was not actually part of our territory. It was almost as if the climate had something to do with it: you might say that, going from north to south, there was a greater acceptance of our mission, i.e., in the south more, in the north less. The reasons had nothing to do with climate: in the Northern Army Group, which had been almost stationary since the winter of 1941, the peace-time influence among the top brass had remained more constant, in other words the atmosphere was conservative; it was different in the southern and central areas, where fresh recruits were continually injecting new ideas. There we were not regarded with the same scepticism. I must say, though, that even among the conservative forces there was no actual disapproval of our work, they just made it clear that they were dubious about our methods. They would have preferred us to shoot the commissars according to military regulations instead of killing them by injection, which we did so as to keep the heads intact. Execution by shooting was the very thing that would have destroyed the heads, and it was the heads that were vital to us.

You are wandering from the subject. What was your procedure? First we looked at the takings of that particular day. Most of those who were supposed to be commissars were not. In one case it would be a noncom, in another an anti-aircraft officer. Anyone who was too outspoken in camp and harangued his men gave the impression of behaving like a commissar. From time to time you would hear the expression "Freemason" commissar. Although it was probably contrary to my orders and meant that later, when I had to carry out the rest of the job, I had the added burden of personal feelings, I frequently had talks with the prisoners, since in my experience this was the best method of selection. The level of education or training gave the best indication of which ones might be commissars. Where there was a certain level of intellectual superiority there was every probability of the man being a commissar.

I don't want to bore you with the finer points of our method. When the selection had been made we took the Jewish-Bolshevist commissars to be measured, this was seldom done the same night, often it wasn't until the next morning, because after the lengthy selection procedure we would be dead beat by the time we returned to our quarters. To save on guard personnel we often took the commissars back to our quarters with us, and this laid us open to the accusation of abusing them homosexually. No such case is known to me—one thing is certain, not even a love affair of this kind could have saved any of the commissars at this stage of proceedings. The local troops were responsible for the bodies that we left behind.

Caution
In future he would refuse to be put in charge of such work or any work like it. He would be extremely careful. And if others did it and he looked on? Caution should be used there too; probably he would do nothing and await developments.

Activity and inactivity
The "Decorations Detachment" was his attempt at activity in his life, and the counterpart to it was now inactivity, so that it was even possible to say: I am a Marxist; but there is nothing one can do.

Road closed to the east
Question: Why don't you go to Eastern Germany?
Answer: They disregard statutory limitations there.

What happened to Professor A. Hirt?
That's a good question. In 1944 I got a postcard from Professor Hirt, when I was in Vienna. In Strassburg the Allies came across the remains of his skull collection—there had not been time to destroy it completely. The Foreign Office asked him for an official reaction to the accusation raised in Swiss newspapers; on April 6, 1945, Hirt promised a prompt reply. Later he disappeared.

Did he have any after-effects from his 1943 wound?
Pain in his right elbow, a periodically recurring inflammation of the ligaments: when that happened he went to a chiropractor for treatment.

No coffee

During the interview a human relationship had developed between B. and the reporter from *L'Humanité*. When the interview was over they would have liked to have a cup of coffee together. This turned out to be impossible. At this hour coffee was not being served in the cafeteria so as not to give the staff an excuse to leave their jobs. And in the cafeteria no one was allowed to sit down. So B. and the interviewer parted without having had a cup of coffee.

Demise of an Attitude:
Chief of Detectives Scheliha

I

In January 1945, Chief of Detectives Scheliha, of the Central Criminal Investigation Department of the German Reich, traveled on official business to the Elbing area. This is what had happened: Since November 1944 a landowner by the name of von Z. had been under investigation by the local police in connection with a murder. For various reasons, however, no charges had been laid. In these final months of the war the authorities were reluctant to take drastic steps against a person enjoying powerful connections. Many local authorities, as well as some senior officials in Elbing, were more inclined to send the suspect to the front. But before proceedings could be terminated in this manner, the files found their way to the Central Criminal Investigation Department in Berlin. Chief of

Detectives Scheliha was instructed to clear up the matter on the spot.

Chief of Detectives Scheliha requested the services of two inspectors, two assistants, a stenographer, and a small police detachment; these were to go on ahead at night by automobile, taking the Fürstenwalde-Schwiebus road. It was his intention to combine the investigation of this case with one last inspection of West Prussia, before that province was also overrun by Russian troops. He followed the advance party by taking the day train to Elbing. That day General Hossbach's troops abandoned the Lötzen barrier and, as a kind of roving pocket, broke through the Russian lines to the west, the Russians having already moved in behind these troops and begun to occupy the province of East Prussia.

It was really a mystery why the local National Socialist government officials did not see to it that the suspect received the punishment he deserved.

II

Scheliha did not remain in the fortified town of Elbing, where the jails were in process of being emptied and many bands of traitors and deserters were being shot; instead he left an inspector behind him, with instructions to keep him posted on the circumstances surrounding the murder and the numerous rumors circulating about events at the front. At the district jail outside Elbing he was informed that, in connection with some local disturbances on the part of foreign workers, there had been a successful prison break. One of the prisoners had been Z., who was being held for questioning. Late that day Scheliha and his staff were driven to Z.'s estate not far from Elbing. He could not understand why this man had not been more strictly guarded.

As could have been foreseen, the suspect was no longer to be found on the estate. Scheliha had some of the farm hands questioned, as well as the priest and the Party leader from the next village. It was established that the suspect had been seen on the grounds for a few hours and had continued his flight in a hunting brake, taking six horses with him (so as always to have two for relief). Scheliha assumed the suspect would avoid heading straight west in the direction of Pomerania or Lower Silesia; he judged that the danger to the suspect of falling into the hands of military police and being taken for a deserter would outweigh any advantage offered by this shorter route. More likely the suspect had fled in a southeasterly curve toward the front, as in this way he had some hope of reaching what had once been Poland (now known as the General Government). The collapse of the Vistula front and the rapid thrust of the Russian armies had created such confusion that the suspect could risk approaching the frontier of the German Reich from that side. Incidentally, at the time the crime was committed there had not been one foreign workers' camp anywhere in the vicinity of the estate, nor was there a single foreign worker, loiterer, or deserter who could have committed the crime. Allusions to roaming foreigners occurred in the statements of every defendant pleading not guilty. Scheliha's attitude to this kind of excuse was basically a sceptical one. He did, however, investigate the possibility of some person other than the suspect having committed the crime. The farm hands were housed in barracks; during working hours they were watched. They had no access to the manor house, the scene of the murder. The information gathered by the inspector left behind at Elbing relating to the background of the Z. murder was communicated by telephone: no specific protection for Z. was apparent, but there was a widespread disinclination to concentrate on this murder at the present time. Party officials had not been consulted. Legal opinion held, among other things, that at the moment the real danger emanated not from people like von Z. but from countless rebellious and desperate bands of individuals who now, toward the end of the war and with the break-through on the Vistula front, saw their chance to revolt. The District Attorney's office likewise took the attitude that in this tense and precarious situation one had no right to kill off one's own countrymen, so to speak; the case must be regarded from the point of view of its consequences. None of these views corresponded to Chief of Detectives Scheliha's opinion.

III

Scheliha needed less than an hour to convince himself of the landowner's guilt. He gave orders for the situation on the premises in which the corpse had been found to be outlined in chalk on the floor, and with the aid of his assistants re-enacted the rather crude crime. One of the laborers was found to be in possession of articles of Z.'s clothing which, as was to be expected, revealed traces of blood. These and other items of evidence were sent to Elbing on a farmcart. Even the awkward fact that the murder had been a particularly brutal one and hence was difficult to ascribe to an educated person of good family (which prompted the thought that perhaps a foreign worker was responsible after all) was satisfactorily explained on the basis of the statements made regarding the personality of the suspect. Actually the suspect—and all those interrogated concurred in this—was a man of high moral standards which in this particular instance had first to be overcome. It was obvious that the mutilation of the guest's head was attributable to the exceptional demands which the landowner normally made of his conscience. It had been an explosion, as it were, of this conscience which, under these particular circumstances, was unable to prevent the crime and thus sought a different outlet in mutilation.

Scheliha left his second inspector behind on the estate with instructions to continue the necessary interrogations until the Russians approached, and then, as the danger increased, to make for Berlin via the fortified town of Elbing. He himself set off by car with his two assistants and the stenographer—to whom en route he dictated a detailed report on information received to date—for the railway junction of Schmielau. From there he hoped to travel south quickly by train or handcar. This way he could expect to intercept the murderer on one of the routes leading south. However, some thirty kilometers before Schmielau he encountered a triple column of military vehicles on the highway. Trucks, three abreast, were driving along the relatively narrow highway, further on there were armored cars, two abreast. Soldiers were clinging to the sides of the armored cars and trucks. These columns, which were trying to reach the fortified town of Elbing, pushed all oncoming traffic—including the Chief of Detectives' vehicles—off the highway. Some dispatch riders cleared a way for the column, which otherwise would have cleared a way for itself; the dispatch riders had instructions to clear everything off the road, and they referred the Chief of Detectives to the next officer. But it was a long time before a senior officer could be found, as it was by no means easy to communicate with an officer in this rapidly moving column and persuade him to dismount. The officer was in danger, if he got off, of losing his unit; he risked his life by jumping off—if he was caught away from his unit he was likely to be court-martialed. The Chief of Detectives was therefore only able to exchange a few words with the officer before the latter jumped back up onto another truck. Scheliha lost several hours during which he could do nothing but wait and hope. Even by taking advantage of the rail connections there was no prospect of apprehending the murderer before he crossed the frontier into Poland.

IV

At the railway junction and fortified town of Schmielau, a garrison town of some 15,000 inhabitants, Chief of Detectives Scheliha found the teletype equipment of the Area Command still intact. He telephoned the inspector whom he had left behind on the suspect's estate and was given the latest results. The murder weapon had been found in the cellars of the manor house, taken to Elbing, and examined there for clues. In addition there were statements from farm hands and local inhabitants.

Via the teletype Scheliha was able to reach a few towns and bases in East Prussia, West Prussia, and the General Government (by this time it could already be called the former General Government). Thus he tried to close in on the murderer who was in the process of escaping somewhere in the nearby woods and fields; in other words, he was improvising a search, even if this method of searching contained considerable gaps. But the demands Scheliha made via the teletype met with indifference, in some cases outright refusal. Under present conditions the search for a single individual was deemed by the local police to be impossible and unwarranted. As if this was a crime of honor! Scheliha sent the following teletype message to the chief of police in Krakow:

Scheliha: In the murder case (then came reference number and additional details) I am encountering obstructionist behavior on the part of the following authorities (there followed a list of authorities). I request that these departments receive appropriate instructions. Scheliha, Chief of Detectives.

Reply: The following departments have received instructions (names of departments followed), remaining departments listed by you can no longer be contacted. The Russians have reached Plock. Instructions given here for continuation of search. Shall we send transportation for you? Reply requested. Schulze, Commissioner-General.

Scheliha: Much obliged. Kindest regards.

Reply: Kind regards.

Scheliha assumed that von Z. would try to reach the German frontier somewhere along the road between Schmielau, Klopau, and Mielczic, the whole section apparently being inadequately patrolled. To get there he would have to reach the Klopau-Mielczic road. Scheliha abandoned the idea of following up the arrest with an inspection of West Prussia. He set off in two cars in the direction of Klopau, accompanied by two assistants, a stenographer, and two police officers.

V

Past a variety of crude scenes of deserters being shot along highways on which the Chief of Detectives' vehicles were unable to display their power to much advantage: on the one hand it seemed that, in the general confusion, one murder more or less was relatively unimportant—besides, it was difficult, if not impossible, to pick out this particular murderer among the hordes of people moving about in various directions; on the other hand, Scheliha could see no valid excuse for discontinuing the pursuit at this stage. He realized that the police—despite the Reich Criminal Investigation Department's excellent and up-to-date organization—were neither in a position nor empowered to cope with such a disastrous state of affairs by police methods, let alone deal successfully with it. They would have had to seize power and erect a virtual police dictatorship side by side with the existing one. All the greater, however, is a police officer's responsibility at the very moment when he is aware that the organization to which he belongs is crumbling to make every effort to carry out his duty and thus, by striving for the utmost police effectiveness, to satisfy—by intent if not in actual fact—the demands of violated justice.

That day Generals Hossbach and Reinhardt, who were in command of the roving pockets in East Prussia, were dismissed and replaced by Generals Schwiethelm and von Müller. In the General Government two field marshals attempted to rally the fleeing German troops at various points. Colonel-General Rendulic, transferred from the defense of Vienna, commandeered a villa for his headquarters and had a palisade built around it. Chief of Detectives Scheliha got as far as the environs of Klopau in his pursuit of the murderer.

VI

The following day the situation in the Plock area deteriorated, Russian troops overran a number of roads leading from north to south more or less parallel to the Vistula. Scheliha decided to dispatch one of his vehicles, with one assistant and the stenographer, in the direction of the German frontier in order not to expose the woman unnecessarily to what might be a dangerous situation close to the front. He himself continued the pursuit toward the south. He had reason to believe he could intercept the hunting brake at an estate near Klopau. Scheliha passed through Klopau (which was surrounded shortly afterward by Russian assault troops) as an appendage to a military transport under the command of a determined lieutenant.

The day after that, in the midst of a traffic jam stretching for many miles, Scheliha was taken prisoner by Russian Guard troops not far from Klopau. He was separated from the police officers and the assistant in his party and, after being held for several days, he and a large number of other prisoners were loaded into boxcars. The files on the Z. case were destroyed when, for reasons which never became clear, the Chief of Detectives' automobile burst into flames during the brief skirmish preceding the capture.

After a hurried visit to the estate of some friends, the murderer Z. had taken—since everything pointed to the Russians not being far off—a secondary road to the west, just beyond the town of Klopau, which appeared passable for his hunting brake. A few days later, following this route, he reached the Reich frontier at Grünberg, in Silesia, this part of the frontier being unguarded at the time. Via Glogau, Kottbus, and Guben and, after abandoning his hunting brake, he managed to get to Schleswig-Holstein, where he was given shelter at the manor house of a large estate. He later moved to the Rhineland and settled there.

Meanwhile Scheliha was traveling in the opposite direction.

Quotation from Kant:

"Even if a bourgeois society should dissolve, with the consent of all its members (e.g., an island-dwelling people should decide to go their separate ways and disperse throughout the world), the last murderer still being held in prison would have first to be executed, in order for each person to receive his just deserts and for the blood-guilt not to attach to the people which has neglected to insist on this punishment; because the people may be considered as participating in this public violation of justice. It is better that one man should die than that a whole people be dragged down; for when justice perishes, the continued existence of human beings on earth becomes valueless."

VII

By the time Scheliha returned from prison camp in 1953, circumstances in Germany had changed. Scheliha refrained from any further pursuit of Z., who now occupied a position in the Rhineland. On June 12, 1961, Scheliha, who had been appointed adviser to the Department of Justice, gave a speech to the Rotary Club in S. on "Justice and Crime."

Excerpts from the discussion:
(Applause)
The President of the Rotary Club: He would like to thank the Honorable Mr. Scheliha for his remarks. Nevertheless he would like to point out that there was a definite appreciation of justice and injustice among Rotarians. Furthermore, there were some things one should not think about too much. *Rotarian Benger-Ribana:* The speaker had called the hussar's tunic an "Attila." The proper name for it was, of course, a "Dolman." The speech contained further examples of the speaker's inaccuracy. But a loosely formulated idea was not even a correct idea when it concerned the unresolved past. *Rot. Plettke:* Legal problems always affected a minority only. *Rot. Barabas:* As a penologist he could not understand the speaker's pessimism. Speaking for himself, he was an optimist in such matters.

(Applause)

There was one important point which Mr. Scheliha had not sufficiently considered: that of mercy. Wherever there was justice, there was also mercy; a justice not enriched with mercy was inconceivable, although in these days, of course, it was necessary to apply stricter standards when dealing with a person applying for a pardon.

(Loud applause)

Basic discussion

Rot. Geibel: He could not imagine that in 1953 the German people had been "without values," as the speaker had maintained. German self-control and German values, in the words of the national anthem, did not perish even in 1945. *Rot. Pils:* If there was blood-guilt, it could not attach to the German people, since the crime had been committed in the province of West Prussia. Hence it attached to Poland. *Rot. Waller:* It was impossible for a society to dissolve, even with the consent of all its members, Kant's example was therefore utopian. *Rot. Henn:* If he might be permitted to speak from his experience in the *Bundestag:* it had been shown repeatedly that, particularly in cases of treason, serious philosophical factors must be taken into consideration, since experience had shown that lax punishment was the very thing which in Kant's sense wrought havoc upon a nation, or rather, wrought havoc from within the nation. *Rot. Glas:* The German people had, after all, insisted on punishment at the time, it was only the apparatus which had failed to function. But Mr. Scheliha himself had recommended moderation. He had cited the example merely on account of his change of attitude. *Rot. Valentin:* He failed to understand why no investigation had been made as to whether or not von Z. had acted in self-defense. *Rot. Mertens:* As far as he knew, Infantry Regiment 71 had been in the environs of Klopau at the time. These troops could have been used to look for the murderer.

Intensified discussion

President: Due to limitations of time, each member's remarks must be restricted to one minute. He therefore asked that comments be kept short. The discussion could continue. *Rot. Lambrecht:* What was meant by "for each person to receive his just deserts"? Philosophically speaking, this must be regarded as a matter of practice. *Rot. Bischof:* Obviously it was a question of action. *Rot. Erb:* And as a doctor one could not do other than support that view. *Rot. Katrin:* All the same, there was no doubt whatever that it was better for one man to die than for a whole people to be dragged down. *President:* True; in principle the Rotary Club was interested in social problems, but this was not strictly speaking a social problem. *Rot. Katrin:* But whether, on the other hand, there was no longer any value in people speaking about the end, that was something he was doubtful about. *Rot. Jacoby:* One must concentrate on the problem itself. *Rot. Schmidthenner:* It was a matter of background and education. *Rot. Glaube:* If he might speak from experience: Frederick II, the King, that is to say, not the Emperor, had once said: The civil servant and the philosopher owed their strength to their detachment from reality. Today, however, he wished to speak not as a civil servant or a philosopher but as a practical man, and practice meant involvement in reality. Who was prepared these days, for example, to risk his life or his liberty for any particular problem of justice? *Rot. Sprengel:* The question of punishment raised by Kant was a very specific and perhaps misleading one. It was possible that a preventive measure on the part of the police was considerably more effective than any subsequent punishment. *Rot. Mainz:* What was required was a state based not on legal procedure but on preventive justice, beginning with the police. Salazar had recognized this long ago. *Rot. Patzak:* To come back to Kant: As a returning prisoner-of-war it had been possible to observe that even without punishment and "values" in the Kantian sense there had still been development and progress. It was very difficult to recall the strange sense of impending disaster prevalent during the final months of the war (the only thing it might be compared to was the mood of deepening twilight in the pre-Christmas period).

On the Love of Justice

Mr. Scheliha: Punishment depended on the mood. In the same way, criminal investigation and crime itself were each dependent on the unity of time and space being maintained. Without a specific atmosphere, neither the crime nor the criminal investigation could succeed. *President:* He wished to thank the speaker for his address. *Rot. Peickert:* He had always considered justice to be one of the most nonsensical ideals. *Rot. Balunga:* He had always been interested in how justice could turn into crime and how crime could evade justice. These aspects should also be borne in mind when examining the problem. *Rot. Pils:* Justice was a totalitarian principle. *Rot. Waller:* It was impossible however, to dispense with justice. The criminologist was the watchdog of legal security, the judge was king of the law. *President:* Would members kindly keep their remarks as brief as possible, as the time for fruitful discussion was limited. *Rot. von Bergmann:* An inordinate love of justice was reminiscent of perversion, in ancient times there had even been defenders of homosexuality. *Rot. Eber:* It was strange that the term justice occurred frequently in texts from classical antiquity. *Rot. Fürbringer:* We must have justice! Without it life would be impossible. *Rot. Schumpeter:* How could he prove it, though? *President:* No interruptions, please: Mr. Fürbringer has the floor.

Conclusion

Rot. Lebsius: The problem discussed today had been most stimulating. The problems involved in the administration of justice had been brought to light in a very productive manner. *Rot. Pichota:* The logical nature of the address had left a great impression. *Rot. Arndt:* At last we have had some plain speaking.

(Lively applause)

President: Now that the discussion had yielded many stimulating ideas, he requested the speaker to make his concluding comments. *Mr. Scheliha:* He thanked the members for this opportunity of speaking to them. *President:* Time was running out, he would like to thank Mr. Scheliha in the name of all those present for his appropriate and enlightening remarks.

(Hearty and prolonged applause)

Fräulein von Posa

I

The young mistress of the manor, Fräulein von Posa, had the gates to the road shut so no one would come into the yard. Later she changed her mind and had the gates opened again. She gave instructions to the kitchen to feed the people who poured into the yard. Smoke hung over the town, the upper layers had been broken off by the wind.

Dr. von Posa was waiting in the drawing room for his coffee. Radio Luxembourg was broadcasting a reasonably good operatic concert. Fräulein von Posa tried to reach the Cathedral dean in town, but this was impossible, all telephone connections with the town having been cut because the enemy was so close. She felt guilty for having wanted to keep the gates to the yard closed. Throughout the day airplanes passed overhead from west to east. As dive bombers approached the estate, Miss Posa ran behind the barns to the air-raid shelter reserved for members of the family. She hardly knew what she was doing as she ran. On the camp cot, which took up most of the room in the small bunker, lay the Pole and Gloria. Miss Posa sat down beside them on the edge of the cot and stopped them from getting up out of embarrassment. Instead she gathered up their articles of clothing which lay strewn around. The young Pole sat between the two women. Gloria began, rather brazenly, to get dressed in front of her sister. Miss Posa busied herself all day with the people who had settled down in the yard and the barns and were being fed. Later on the chairman of the Rural District Council arrived with some of his men and resumed the search for the runaway Pole. They found him this time, he had become careless and was wandering around behind the barns. The chairman of the Rural District Council had him handcuffed and interrogated him.

Toward evening American tanks approached the town, whence the long-drawn-out sound of a siren was to be heard. Miss Posa was occupied with the laborers and foreign workers coming in from the fields in small groups. They were avid for news. By evening the young foreign worker, Gloria's Pole, had disappeared. During the night two women who were in labor were brought in from the town, and Miss Posa had to persuade her father to accept them: he could not afford to turn them down—but he had got into the habit of letting himself be persuaded. The births also kept Gloria busy, for she had to cut the umbilical cord, the only thing Dr. von Posa could not bring himself to do. This was liberation day.

II

After it became certain that the Pole would not return, Miss Posa gradually relaxed. The night following the arrival of the Allies she could not fall asleep, so she got dressed again and began to tidy up the house. She collected the numerous crosses and statuettes of Jesus which were in the house and made her uneasy, and put them all together in one spot. She was afraid to see these objects in their accustomed places. She desired passionately to be good again. She saw incredulously that there were circumstances which made it impossible to be good but which offered no compensation. What was to happen? She suffered a crisis during the night and prayed (crouched in an armchair). Then she wept until she fell asleep.

Continence

She could have taken this young foreign worker for her lover—he had access to the manor because only in the manor could he be safely hidden. Why didn't she take him? Her continence drove the man into the arms of her little sister, whom she ought to have protected better.

Reaction to the disappearance
of the young foreign worker

Miss Posa shed some of the malaise of the last few days when she was sure she would not find him again; nevertheless she looked for him till it was dark. She drove in her car to the various foreign workers' quarters, where freedom celebrations were gradually getting under way, and asked for him. He had not been seen anywhere.

Vampire father

Ever since these glorious sunny spring days had set in, she had had a vague, passionate desire which could have been channeled in any direction, but the only outlet for this good will was her father, who appropriated what he could get of it. He exploited her in his practice, where she sterilized instruments for him, or he sent her on errands to neighboring estates or into town: to shop for specialties at the delicatessen stores.

Dr. von Posa

Ernst, born 1886, studied medicine, became a doctor like his father before him. Everyone prophesied a brilliant career for Ernst von Posa. In 1914 became deputy superintendent of Field Hospital No. 3 in Lemberg, a clearing station for the wounded of the rapidly retreating 3rd army of General of the Cavalry von Brudermann. Posa was caught in the Przemysl trap, where he had managed to salvage portions of his Lemberg hospital. Within a few days the encircled stronghold of Przemysl was doomed. As a prisoner-of-war of the Russians, Posa was exchanged via Denmark for captured Russian doctors. In 1916 he visited the battlefield of September 16, 1914, at the Oise, where two of Posa's brothers were buried. Had the Zouaves cut out their eyes?

The war over, his only desire was for the "finer things of life." Visited Mallorca and Ibiza in 1921; Tunis and Greece in 1923; traveled through Portugal and Spain in 1928; married Brigitte von D. in 1920, divorced six years later. Various Mediterranean voyages in 1932, 1935, 1936, 1937, 1939 (in the spring), including Corfu. Country practice and maternity home at the Posa estate. Extremely sensitive to cold. Since Przemysl unable to tolerate hunger, hence his daily schedule punctuated by numerous small meals. Short-tempered with patients. Plays the violin.

Turning-point

As far back as February, Fräulein von Posa had been hoping for a turning-point in her personal relations and intentions. She noticed that something inside her was getting ready. She was familiar with these presentiments from previous occasions, and calculated that after the nadir of the last few years there was bound to be an upward trend.

Corpse recovery detail

For a long time Miss Posa found no opportunity of doing anything except: feeding people who would otherwise have got their food somewhere else, until she received an offer to take charge of a corpse recovery detail. She accepted this assignment and with the aid of her men (farm laborers, workers supplied by the civic authorities) searched the ruined town for corpses. On the third day, fortified with brandy to enable them to endure the stench, they found a cellar under the rubble. It contained sixty bodies. In addition they found isolated corpses, bodies charred to the size of an arm, also some that had merely been buried under rubble and therefore looked normal, all of which they transported to mass graves supplied by the civic authorities. Fräulein von Posa asked for one week's leave for her men during which she wanted to clear a bombed church with them. This was refused at the insistence of the health authorities. During this time Miss Posa often thought of the young Pole.

Search for something good

After the recovery detail had also cleared up the civic theater site, it was disbanded and not put to work rebuilding churches, as Fräulein von Posa had requested. So she roamed the streets searching for something good to do. But her efforts with the military occupation authorities merely led to misunderstandings, and she was unable to clarify these because she lacked the necessary experience. There was no market for what she had in mind. For a month she observed signs of pregnancy on her body. But a pregnancy was impossible. Gloria confessed to her that she had committed an indiscretion with the Pole. She talked to Gloria about the Pole and kissed her sister when they talked about him. After their conversation she felt an even stronger desire for something good.

III

The Posa family migrated from the Netherlands to Jülich-Cleve in the seventeenth century. Living in this province the family became part of Prussia. During the first siege of Mainz, a Lieutenant von Posa, under the eyes of his Elector, prevented the slaughter of a civilian in the village of Bretzenheim. In 1793 a member of the Pomeranian branch of the von Posa family went over to the French revolutionary troops and was executed by a firing squad after the occupation of Paris in 1815. In 1848 J.H. von Kirchheim, Vice-President of the Superior Assize Court in Ratibor from 1836 to 1851 (his mother was a von Posa), canceled the warrant for the arrest of Count Reichenbach. The King of Prussia wrote to him: Do not understand ruling, herewith express my dissatisfaction. Von Kirchheim was given five years' leave of absence. As a deputy in the Prussian Diet, von Kirchheim raised constitutional objections to measures of this kind. While on his way back he was forcibly retired on grounds of discreditable behavior. The four Posas then in Prussian service as magistrates and army officers resigned their posts. Later generations of the Posa family provided doctors only. In 1871 it was Surgeon-General Franz von Posa who drew the attention of Lieutenant-General von Voigt-Rhetz to the butcher Steinmetz during the battle of St. Privat. The following day Steinmetz was replaced by another military commander.

Eight von Posas and von Kirchheims took part in World War I. The eccentric advance of the Austro-Hungarian armies to the north beyond Lemberg cost most of them their lives. They fell as Prussian liaison and medical officers in the armies of Brudermann and Dankl and as members of the Prussian auxiliary force Woersch. Two other von Posas fell shortly afterward in the west, after accomplishing nothing. The only one to survive World War I was the shell-shocked Ernst von Posa on the Posa estate in northern Hesse. During the next few years the Posa family suffered a crisis. The surviving and younger generations of Posas: the same mouth, shadows around the mouth, the same inquisitive eyes, dark golden-brown, prematurely graying hair, temples throbbing when excited, veins at the temples—just like the Posas around 1700, around 1800, around 1900, but now in a crisis.

IV

What is good (bonum)?

Not the Fatherland, Europe—which Europe? The soothing of pain, misfortune, bring no relief. To abstain from wrongdoing—what does that mean? A Posa commits no wrongs. The truth? Tell it to whom? Continence—no. What, then, is good? The family estates? Yes. But that cannot be all.

Lieutenant von Hacke (a Posa on his mother's side)

Love for the inherited estates near Brunswick was the undoing of Ernst von Hacke. Returning as a major from World War I (last in Hamburg, 1919, liquidation of artillery horse stocks at a considerable profit for the Treasury), he hoped to acquire the funds necessary for the maintenance of the estates by working without pay in the banking firm of Traeger, Pelckert & Co. (relations of his wife). Tips from banking friends in Munich prompted him to enter into speculations in which he lost additional moneys. The encumbered estates were placed under trusteeship. From 1928 to 1930 Major von Hacke studied singing in Hanover. His first instructor, court singer Merkel von Karonin, had expressed himself optimistically about his career in this field. Von Hacke threw himself into this new life, which seemed to offer rich spoils. In the following years the name Hacke appeared in the musical programs of Coburg, Halberstadt, Kottbus, Torgau, Brandenburg, and Danzig, but never prominently. Von Hacke avoided the Brunswick area. In 1935 Hacke was recalled to the Wehrmacht. On September 1, 1935, he took up his duties at the War Ministry in Berlin with the rank of lieutenant-colonel. Posted in remote headquarters, he missed the Polish and Western campaigns. He saw his chance of saving the estates if he distinguished himself in this war.

In 1941 friends obtained one of the then most effective implements of the army for him: the 2nd Lower Saxon Panzer regiment. This fine regiment went with the 44th armored unit to northern Russia. Fair Saxon craniums looked out of well-equipped tank turrets. Special apparatus of all kinds was at his disposal. As commanding officer of this weapon von Hacke could, theoretically speaking, count on being decorated: even the Knight's Cross with Oak Leaves seemed within reach. The decorations would have freed him from all anxiety, for it was improbable that such a distinguished soldier would later be left at the mercy of his debts. However, before it had come to a single engagement with the enemy the regiment's vehicles entered a wide expanse of swampland. The regiment had to be escorted back in the midst of the offensive. One week later, the regiment, now being utilized on a different front sector, saw itself abandoned by the accompanying infantry regiments. En route to Leningrad its flanks were attacked right and left by the enemy. The Panzers had no choice except to retreat. Von Hacke stood weeping with his officers beside the plank road, watching the tanks, mounted with grenadiers, rumbling back; meanwhile from the sides, desperate defense action on the part of the machine-gun units, who were trying to give the regiment a chance.

Winter and spring were likewise devoid of success. Hacke's Panzer regiment, which had hitherto operated independently, was reincorporated in a Panzer division. For a time von Hacke fought in vain in the Crimea. Because of these failures Hacke-Posa did not take part in the officers' conspiracies of 1943/44. In Croatia he was given a gendarmerie regiment which, however, had to grapple with insurmountable problems. Even extraordinary success could no longer have led to promotion or decorations in this remote theater of war. A liaison during the furlough in the Reich capital caused new debts to accumulate there. At that point an English air raid mistakenly destroyed the object of all these efforts: the Herford estate. Hacke, now promoted to colonel, knew nothing of this when the request of one of his friends reached him to take part in the relief of Budapest. So he advanced with his unit on Budapest. His attacks from the southwest confused the attackers and the attacked; it was expected the city would be relieved from Lake Balaton. After two days the regiment, mentioned specifically in the dispatches of the Supreme Command, withdrew once more to the Yugoslavian border.

For a variety of reasons this stroke of luck came too late. (The indebtedness of the von Hacke estates did not improve until the currency reform.) Von Hacke took over command of a divisional headquarters in the Chositz valley. The division expected from Greece, of which this headquarters was supposed to assume command, never materialized. The staffs of Hacke, Fehn, and Kobe, all of whom were in the valleys of former Herzogovina trying to decide whether to break through to the American lines or surrender to the partisans, negotiated with partisan leaders in Krtic-Chositz. During the night the partisan leaders fled, believing themselves to be in danger. A heavily armed tank column, carrying the staffs of Fehn, Kobe, and Hacke, reached the American lines near Klagenfurt but were turned back. This was no laughing matter. A few days later von Hacke, Fehn, and Kobe were executed.

Baroness von Posa

During the night of January 2 to 3, 1945, Baroness von Posa was relieved of her conscience. The conscience was an ordinary cash box containing the von Posa family jewels. Erika von Posa had sent the cash box by registered mail from the Posa estate in eastern Germany to Nuremberg, as soon as friends in the Supreme Command had informed her that the Russians were approaching Posa. The cash box arrived safely in Nuremberg and, as agreed at the outbreak of the war, was being held by a pharmacist's family at the "Golden Star" (as the venerable pharmacy was called). The Baroness herself held out too long on the estate. She and her farm wagons got caught up among retreating German troops. In the twenties she had driven to Berlin with these wagons and farm hands from the old Posa estate near Stolpe and had supervised functions of the German People's Party in Berlin. Now during the first days of snow she lost her farm hands, the foreign workers, and the wagons. Her own wagon was pushed off the side of the road by armored vehicles. After she was flung out a wagon wheel rolled across her shins. Soldiers carried her on a stretcher to a field hospital. She turned up in Nuremberg as a cripple who could only get about in a wheelchair, that is unless she wanted to crawl. During the night of January 2 to 3, 1945, the city of Nuremberg was attacked by Allied bombers. The "Golden Star" was hit by incendiaries and high-explosive bombs. Baroness von Posa and the owners of the building spent the hours of the attack in the lower vaults of the "Star." Five fully finished basement levels contained medical supplies, alcohol, and dressings. When the occupants of the cellar noticed smoke seeping in, they broke through the bricked-up entrance that led to the catacombs of the old section of Nuremberg. With her conscience pressed against her aging body, Erika von Posa tried to crawl to the gap in the wall through which the owners had escaped. The bricked-up entrance was separated from the cellar level by an eighteen-inch threshold. The Baroness fell from this sill into the catacomb passage, which was considerably lower. Her poorly mended shinbones broke. Some looters turned up out of the darkness after she had been shouting for help for some hours and took away her sole possession, the cash box with her conscience.

The Baroness spent the years 1945 to 1948 in the Gartenstadt refugee camp in northern Bavaria, where the Nuremberg air-raid victims had first been taken. Her nephew, André von Teck, returned from a Russian prisoner-of-war camp in 1949. He took the Baroness to live with him in his home in Wiesbaden. The cash box turned up later at a jeweler's; the Baroness denied it was hers. Her leg bones grew together again, Baroness von Posa declined to move about to any appreciable extent.

Police Commissioner von Kirchheim

Von Kirchheim's way of looking at things (he was born in 1906) was that of logic. The logical way of looking at things corresponds to that of internal administration. It regards the state as a machine: however, this leads not to a simplified view but to inventiveness, if this machinery of administration and police is to be adapted to individual requirements and realities. In 1923 von Kirchheim entered the service of the Prussian Internal Administration. In 1929 he switched to the police branch. 1933 found him in Breslau investigating a murder. On January 28 Kirchheim ordered the arrest of the perpetrators, who were Brownshirts. Within a few days Group Leader Heines was made Chief of Police in Breslau and Governor of Silesia. On February 6 trade union leaders were shot in their apartments. After the March elections, Commercial Counselor Jägerlein, together with a member of the local district council, was found shot. Two labor leaders were found dead on March 16. Brownshirts appeared in the apartment of Secretary Lindau and started shooting. When the journalist König left a house in the Breitenstrasse one evening, his face was slashed with a razor. In these cases von Kirchheim appeared at the scene of the crime accompanied by reliable police officials. To the wife of a trade union leader who requested protection for various trade union members, he replied: What do you expect us to do? We can hardly protect ourselves.

What is the meaning of bravery at a time when all that matters is not to be trampled to death? Von Kirchheim did not find the right moment for the traditional brave deed. In 1941 von Kirchheim was appointed inspector for the border area between Lithuania and East Prussia. There were cases of overlapping authority to be cleared up here. Von Kirchheim produced a report containing important suggestions for manpower and material savings in these border areas; moreover, the report was of basic significance for other border areas where overlapping occurred. Later in Allenstein he heard that incidents had taken place in the border area during his tour of inspection about which he had not been told. In the "weeding out process" there were 201 dead in Garsden, 288 in Krottingen, 191 in Polangen, 255 in Taurroggen, 322 in Georgenburg, 192 in Wladislawa, 68 in Mariampol, 230 in Wirballen, 150 in Calvaria, 300 in Wilkowischen, and an undetermined number in Szewekzwie and Vebirzewiai. Those were murders. Von Kirchheim went to Berlin and lodged complaints with the Ministry of the Interior. For the time being he was given no further assignment. Later he was given a police regiment in the Caucasus for whose achievements he was awarded the Knight's Cross. His deplorable behavior at the Ministry of the Interior appeared to have been forgotten. But then von K. was executed in the fall of 1944. It subsequently turned out that the occasion for adopting the attitude which cost him his life had been ill chosen, for the excesses in the border areas had already been stopped from another source. But which moment, which situation, from among the onslaught of events since 1933 would have been a more appropriate one for Kirchheim's intervention?

The ambitious Gerda von Posa-Esebeck

Cousin Gerda was found guilty by a criminal court in Kattowitz of impersonating a Red Cross nurse (actually she was under age and was not permitted to wear a Red Cross uniform). She had been recognized from the description in Nos. 1044–1046 of the German Police Gazette, according to which was of slight build, sixteen years old, and carried papers proclaiming her to be twenty-two. She wore an Iron Cross Class II to which she was not entitled. The officials identified her from the description in the German Police Gazette. A spurious Red Cross nurse had turned up in Rottenburg, Munich, Gleiwitz, Guben, Leipzig, Jena, Hanover, Kreiensen, Halberstadt, Goslar, Strasbourg, Essen, Freiburg, Schneidemühl, Danzig, Allenstein, and Litzmannstadt. It was for this Red Cross nurse that Gerda von Posa was mistaken.

She was convicted of a number of misdemeanors and sentenced to two years in prison.

The unfortunate First Lieutenant von Posa

His promotion to the rank of first lieutenant nearly came to nought as a result of his argumentative streak. In the presence of Field Marshal von Reichenau he criticized the Army's training methods. The Field Marshal laughed. Since the officers who were present interpreted it as a benevolent laugh, the first lieutenant was not demoted to the rank of second lieutenant. A few weeks later young Posa found himself taking part in the skirmish at Feodosia on the Black Sea. The term battle is permissible where the number of dead on both sides amounts to 1,200; at Feodosia sixteen soldiers fell on the Russian side and 240 on the German. A heavy Russian cruiser appeared in Feodosia harbor during the night of December 26 to 27, 1941. They trained their naval searchlights on the German gun emplacements. Later, 23,000 men landed, touching off the well-known crisis on the Kerch Peninsula which cost Corps Commander von Sponeck his life and the 46th Infantry Division its honor. It was in these unfortunate circumstances that von Posa, who came through the fighting alive, found himself involved. No further reformist ideas were accepted from him. In 1943 he went over to the Russians.

Fräulein von Posa

Born March 28, 1922, on the Posa estate, the daughter of Dr. E. von Posa: Nata von Posa. Charged with the care of her younger sister Gloria von Posa. Searching for some good she can do; as the spring of 1945 approaches, turning-point imminent, great expectations combine with the new year. Frequent attendance at church, though the church building is burnt out and only a temporary shed is available. If she had been asked unexpectedly what she really meant by "being good," she would not have known how to answer. She was a small part of the confused Posa family. But she was sure she would think of an answer. It had to be soon. It had to be this spring. She prayed fervently.

V

In the fall of 1945 N. von Posa became the business representative of the Care Parcel organization for the district of Hesse. This had some remote connection with being good, at least it was a charitable enterprise. She was paid a suitable annual salary. In exchange she sacrificed the much-hoped-for turning-point. Sacrifices of this kind were familiar to her: what it amounted to was that she capitulated once more, as she had done at various times in the past: it would have been foolish not to take advantage of the opportunity.

A Change
of Career

I

We who are new, nameless, difficult to understand, we, the prematurely born of a future as yet untested—for a new end we need a new means: a new health, a stronger, shrewder, tougher, bolder, gayer health than any the world has ever seen.
F. Nietzsche, *The Gay Science*

In 1938 Schwebkowski was taken out of Grade 6 and placed in the National Socialist Institute for Political Training at Ballenstedt, NAPOLA for short. The normal continuity of discipline in the home, grade school, and high school was interrupted. A number of such ahistorical persons grew up in various NAPOLAS scattered throughout Germany, including Schwebkowski from 1936 to 1942. In 1943 Schwebkowski

159

joined the Peter Freytag Division of the S.S. which was being organized in northern Greece. In the process of being assembled the cadres of this division, however, were reassigned to three army divisions. The immediate restoration of these divisions was given top priority, they were to be thrown into the threatened southern Ukraine—without the S.S. Division. During his training Schwebkowski quarreled with an army officer. He escaped from the military prison because he faced the possibility of execution. In the uniform of a first lieutenant he attached himself to army transports and crossed the Balkans heading north. His original plan had been to get through to his old school in Ballenstedt. But since the number of military police increased as the troop trains in which he was traveling approached the old Austrian frontier he slowed down his journey in Laibach and continued on by other trains toward the southeast.

In the fall of 1943 Schwebkowski met Francesca B. in Sofia, in a Rumanian army billet. Schwebkowski became involved in business deals. When the Russians appeared in Sofia in 1944, Schwebkowski, who had taken off his uniform of a first lieutenant, was denounced by business friends. As a result he lost B., whom he never saw again. He was taken to the transit camp not far from Odessa. To a rootless person such as Schwebkowski the countryside cannot mean as much as it does to previous generations, for there is no piece of land that Schwebkowski wishes to own and without the urge to ownership there can be no pleasure in a beautiful landscape. This void is filled by one's relationship to the part of the country in which personal decisions have been made. The countryside between Kilomea and Odessa is therefore one of two homes for Schwebkowski, because one of two decisions affecting his life took place here.

Today Schwebkowski regards his decision in spring 1945

to escape from the transit camp near Odessa and get through to the legendary American lines in Kärnten as a wrong one. In retrospect he feels his chances would have been better had he adjusted himself to prison work. In that case he might have been back in Sofia before 1948, possibly as a Russian or Rumanian citizen. Until that time he would have found B. still living in Sofia.

II

Let us chase those Heaven-darkeners,
World-obscurers, cloud-gatherers,
Let us brighten the Empyrean!
Let us roar—O spirit
Of free spirits,
My happy soul roars like
The storm itself.

F. Nietzsche, *The Gay Science*

In 1945 many young people were looking forward to a splendid freedom, a new beginning. In June 1945 the commander of an American armored division heading back west had set up headquarters in Halle. His measures kept the local authorities hopping. Thanks to this commander, a teachers' training college opened in Halle as early as June 1945. The courses here continued when the Russians occupied Halle. It was at this teachers' college that Schwebkowski received his training. His hopes in the boundless possibilities of a teaching career were still intact. He took it for granted that the easiest way to regain the lost dream of the years 1936 to 1942 was as a teacher. From 1946 to 1949 Schwebkowski taught in the Halle and Magdeburg areas. In 1950 he accepted a teaching post at a private school in the southwest of the Federal Republic of Germany. In 1952 the school board in Freiburg discovered that all Schwebkowski had was some kind of war-time matric and a 1946 high school teaching diploma which, according to the regulations laid down by the Ministry of Cultural Affairs, could not be recognized. His appointment was revoked. But this did not cause Schwebkowski to abandon his plan. He registered as a student at the University of Marburg. Marburg-on-the-Lahn is a long, serpentine town coiling around a hill. It is hemmed in by the serpentine highway leading along the valley of the River Lahn from Kassel in the north to Giessen in the south. Steep slopes on both sides prohibit detours, permit walks. Schwebkowski sought to alleviate the dreariness of study by taking up music, but the lost dream of the years 1936 to 1942, which is a living thing, is not to be replaced by an evening at the piano. Dagmar Grothusen, a married woman, tried, so to speak, to lure Schwebkowski into a ravine. She saw a chance of utilizing his strength to bring about a change in her matrimonial captivity. She probably counted on Schwebkowski helping her if she relied on him sufficiently. It is difficult to escape such a situation when it occurs in desolate surroundings with no hope for the foreseeable future. Only the conviction that a teaching career could restore something of the lost NAPOLA era induced Schwebkowski to invest so much in his studies. From what was in itself a meaningless embrace, Frau Grothusen released Schwebkowski too late. Frau Grothusen did not want to have an abortion. Schwebkowski would have provided funds which he had just received from an inheritance. So, in order to escape the tiresome demands of this woman, Schwebkowski transferred to Munich, where he obtained his teaching diploma.

III

In those days every available new teacher in Bavaria, whether elementary, vocational, or secondary school, was being sent to the Aschaffenburg area, where there was an acute shortage in every category. The proximity of the province of Hesse, which enjoyed a greater potential of new teachers, pointed up a certain deficiency in Bavaria's educational system. Schwebkowski found himself among the teachers provisionally assigned to this area. He had to do some probationary teaching in a number of schools, sometimes in the presence of a member of the school board who would assist him with advice. In Schwebkowski's background the cogwheel of discipline was missing. Clashes with authority ensued here just as they had during Schwebkowski's military training in northern Greece. In Schwebkowski's opinion the preparatory period at university and the probationary period in schools were too long-drawn-out, he was also coming to believe less and less that his investment was balanced by even the slightest hope. After receiving his final diploma Schwebkowski moved to the North Rhineland and Westphalia area where (with greater territorial scope) he hoped for more favorable working conditions. From 1958 to 1960 Schwebkowski taught in various schools in this region. He gathered impressions, found little to look forward to, but did not yet abandon his earlier hopes. In 1960 he met de Martin, Chief School Administrator, and a friendship sprang up with this busy man, who was provided with an official car. De Martin tried to talk Schwebkowski into joining the Department of Education.

The aspirations Schwebkowski cherished and wanted to put into practice as a teacher were regarded by de Martin as utopian, even somewhat fascist. He pointed out that Schwebkowski never used the term National Socialist or National Socialism: he spoke either of Hitler or Fascism. Schwebkowski had still not adjusted, he was still animated by the rhythms of the years 1935 to 1945. De Martin did his best to persuade him. After Schwebkowski had changed: from a schoolboy to a National Socialist, from a National Socialist to an aspirer after freedom, from an aspirer after freedom to an undergraduate, from an undergraduate to a conformist (so far always lured on by one goal), he found himself face to face with someone who denied that a single one of the things he had stood for was real. Schwebkowski did not believe him.

IV

In fall 1961 every teacher in D. was deeply shocked by Willett's arrest. Willett, who taught Latin, Greek, and History, was the same age as Schwebkowski. Late one afternoon he had been seen in a deserted map room of the Grillparzer High School in the company of a young girl, the sixteen-year-old student P. Gnade. Nobody could offer a satisfactory explanation for their presence in the rarely used room; the statements of both pupil and teacher remained ambiguous. The school board tried to make light of the incident and suppress discussion of it by teachers in the city. The girl's parents, however, lost no time in filing suit. Before the case could come to trial in D., Schwebkowski managed to get his friend Willett, whose passport had been confiscated by the police, to Italy. But Willett, who had had no training in escape methods, was arrested in Florence and extradited to the Federal Republic of Germany. Had Willett really committed an offense? For Schwebkowski (and for his champion de Martin, who was trying to win Schwebkowski over) this was completely irrelevant. Naturally they denied the facts as presented by police and parents; but quite apart from that an altogether different principle was involved: whether they were in a position to protect one of their own kind in an awkward dilemma such as this. It was a question of power, of whether education is a power, of whether protection is possible for education as a body.

V

Conversation with de Martin

The scientific principles which are the source of the individual maxims of school administration are kept constantly in mind by the School Board, and it serves the Department by being able to supervise and properly appreciate its various methods along general lines; moreover, it performs those of the Department's duties which require free time for scholarship and which cannot flourish amid the distractions of day-to-day business. Wilhelm von Humboldt

The telephone in the Chief Administrator's office was busy all morning. There was a short time when it was free, but then the school switchboard was overloaded. When Schwebkowski was able to dial his friend's office during the lunch hour, the secretary, who did not know who Schwebkowski was, told him de Martin had just left the office. Unnerved by the dialing and the long wait (at times he had used public telephones), Schwebkowski omitted to satisfy himself personally that de Martin was not in his office. He would have found the Chief Administrator still there.

In the afternoon Schwebkowski was told that de Martin could be found in the Parliament building. Schwebkowski searched the building where the Provincial Ministry of Cultural Affairs was in session. It so happened, however, that de Martin was engaged in conveying the greetings of the Minister of Cultural Affairs and the Mayor to a teachers' conference elsewhere. Time was running out for Schwebkowski. Schwebkowski met de Martin that evening in the lobby of the Rhine Hall. As soon as de Martin saw his friend, his expression turned into a friendly grimace; he was well known for the speed of this transformation process: one moment a certain ministerial superiority, next the kind and helpful expression of a friend. He was still hoping to recruit Schwebkowski for the Department of Education. This was why he promised to speak to the Deputies Fuhr and Semmler about the Willett case. De Martin ran into friends who were more important than Schwebkowski. Later on he spoke to the above-named Deputies, who had come to the reception; but since de Martin had a number of more urgent matters to discuss, he did not concentrate on the Willett case. The Deputies forgot the name he had mentioned almost immediately. If de Martin had made a greater effort, the outcome would presumably have been no different. That is probably why de Martin did not concentrate sufficiently on this case. However, in order to utilize the slim chance of a stroke of luck in the Willett case (e.g., that the District Attorney's office would drop the case) for winning over Schwebkowski, he did at least mention the case briefly, so as to be able to say he had spoken to Fuhr and Semmler about it, for de Martin habitually spoke the truth in such matters, since untruths lead to needless entanglements. The next day Schwebkowski was unable to reach de Martin. The Chief Administrator had gone on a tour of inspection to Münster, Cologne, Duisburg, and Essen, and was not expected back until the end of the week. De Martin had left a message with his secretary that he had spoken to the Deputies. De Martin could not be reached while he was away. It did not take long for Schwebkowski to grasp the fact of de Martin's inaccessibility.

Willett is handed over at the Brenner Pass

Could the Austrian border officials have prevented the transit of the prisoner Willett from Italy to the Federal Republic? The Austrian colonel in charge of the border checkpoint at the Brenner Pass advised against it. Opposite him sat Willett, wearing a shabby raincoat, exhausted from the strain of traveling under guard. Schwebkowski, who had arrived at the border during the night, tried to save his friend. But a refusal to permit the transit would merely have resulted in the return of the prisoner to Milan. From there Willett would have been flown to Germany. The expenses of the flight would have had to been borne by Willett. The Austrian border officials could therefore not save Willett either.

The example of Ambassador von O.

In the Third Reich there was a certain Ambassador von O. who later helped to salvage the art treasures of Rome. He was not a National Socialist. But the position he held was of use to the National Socialists. He held it so as to be able to continue protecting friends and colleagues. His signature, his personality, his secret opposition, sheltered the policy of the National Socialists. In the end he lost most of his friends and protégés, later even his post. After the war he was court-martialed. The Ambassador's permanently trumped-up position is a prototype for Schwebkowski; it indicates the borderline: As soon as it is no longer possible to protect one's friends, the time has come to change jobs.

Brief Summary

As water is conducted along a strand of wool from a full glass into an empty one.   Socrates

The educational methods of a society which actually does not desire education: fourteen subjects are spread over nine, maximum twelve years. Everything is repeated twice. What is learned at home is repeated in class. What is learned in three months is tested at intervals. If you pay attention you get through the educational institution without a scratch.

The pedagogue humbled by the Customs
In 1918 the Soviet teacher Makarenko, accompanied by a group of eight juvenile delinquents, occupied a remote former Tsarist barracks in which there was nothing but an ax, which they could use to kill each other. They did not kill each other because they needed one another.

Returning to Berlin from a class outing with his pupils, Schwebkowski got into an argument with the West German Customs officials at Helmsted. He had allowed the boys to take along papers and books printed in East Berlin. The Customs officials confiscated these; under the sharp eyes of the boys, who missed nothing, the teacher proved no match for ignorant officials. Copious correspondence later ensued, as the jurisdictional aspects of Schwebkowski's resistance could not immediately be clarified. In another instance, the school board objected to a class of sixteen-year-olds reading Jean-Paul Sartre's *The Wall*. In yet another instance, an outing promised by the teacher was not approved because of the risk involved in transporting the boys, the permissible quota of student accidents in that district having exceeded the maximum level. Because he could foresee similar obstacles, Schwebkowski refrained from even suggesting a considerable number of other projects.

Will the teaching profession ever become the leading profession?
All these elements: scholarly distinction, excellent professional standards, a commensurate salary, an outlook based on an innate dignity, combined with the considerate treatment ac-

corded the teaching staff, have surrounded this profession with a respect and recognition in society which it had not hitherto possessed and which redounds very much to its advantage. Hence a well-qualified young secondary school teacher is, socially speaking, perfectly secure, he is on a par with civil servants of other categories, even the most highly respected, and every year offers examples of marriages between such teachers and daughters from families of the highest-ranking civil servants.

Friedrich Thiersch, *Public Education, I,* p. 460, ca. 1840

In actual practice, the position to which modern social developments entitle the teacher meets with considerable difficulties. A teacher lacks the freedom to shape his life in a manner in keeping with his function in society, and the independence and freedom of choice a treasury official has is far greater these days than that of a school teacher or school principal. If senior civil servants and the army officers represented the highest social level in the state at one time, it might be said that today, to use the metaphor of a bygone mode of thought, the teaching profession has attained the highest social level in the modern world.

Hellmut Becker, *Quantity and Quality,* 1962

Qualified teachers are paid according to the same scale as university laboratory assistants—what is the connection between the teaching profession and a civil service salary scale? Teachers need a sabbatical year every seven years in order to bring themselves up-to-date—who gives them this free time? The problem of education and thus of teacher-training are the greatest political concern of our time—but how many people take these matters seriously? The teaching profession needs dedication—but is it permitted to have it?

Quest over which Willett tripped

Narrow, brown back—not inviting to sexual intercourse. Bony and shivering under the skin—attractive to the initiated, moving to teachers. This was also destroyed many centuries ago in the Albigenses. The door to the seldom used map room was flung open by the witness and subsequent informer: no power in the entire realm of culture can save the exposed teacher now.

Schwebkowski abandons a faith

The Willett case finally convinces Schwebkowski of something of which he was partly convinced before—that the society in which we live has no use for education, for invention, for intellectual activity and quest. If this were not so, certain forces would come into play which could be employed in Willett's favor.

Are you not conscious in such figures as Spinoza, for example, of something profoundly enigmatic, puzzling, and mysterious? Do you not see the drama being played out here, the steady draining of color—*the ever more ideally interpreted desensualization? Do you not sense in the background some long-concealed vampire who begins with the senses and is finally left with, finally leaves, dry bones?*

F. Nietzsche, *The Gay Science*

Around 1800 apprehensive people started channeling Germany's intellectual life. Ideality replaced power, sublimation replaced criticism, legal history outdistanced law, attention was focused on philosophy rather than practice, on history of art rather than construction. Hegel was summoned to Berlin by the Government to divert young people's minds from dangerous practical ideals. The pacification was successful. Of what use is a rebellion of the intellect when organized intellect opposes rebellion? Docile faculties let themselves be bullied and staffed by pacifiers and themselves became pacified; schools organized along military lines trained the noncommissioned officers and officers who won the battles of Königgrätz and Sedan and lost those between 1914 and 1918. What can the years of democratic work from 1923 to 1928 (preceded by inflation, followed by economic crisis) achieve against a hundred and fifty years of tradition? How quickly can tradition blot out a momentary hiatus in history between 1933 and 1945? Under the circumstances Schwebkowski decided there was no point in being a teacher.

VI

Compromise is no basis for education, for education demands courage and resolution: its purpose is to give a direction to life. Rahmenplan, p. 33

The final conversation between the two friends Schwebkowski and de Martin had to be postponed several times because of de Martin's heavy schedule. It took place at de Martin's home. De Martin had suggested this so he could exert his purely personal influence on Schwebkowski: in the hope that Schwebkowski's dissatisfaction with a teaching career might prompt him to join the Department of Education. He enticed him with visions of a higher salary scale. Frau de Martin served tea and joined in the attempt at persuasion.

In the spring of 1962 Schwebkowski changed careers. He joined a Düsseldorf real estate firm. Here he was finally able to put to use the money he had received from the inheritance.

Manfred Schmidt

I THE CARNIVAL

Time: six P.M. The bells ring out over the loudspeakers through the empty halls. Loudspeakers have been installed in the large foyer and blare across the wide staircases.

1

Trucks arrive bringing cardboard walls, churning up the snow and slush.

2

The checkroom attendants settled into their small quarters. They take part in the carnival from the safe harbor of their work.

3

The watchmen of the Patrol & Security Service in their policeman-type overcoats have hermetically sealed off the building. They are still searching the basement for loopholes in the security system.

4

Green cartons of liquor are delivered and distributed to the various floors. An out-of-town company tries to smuggle in deliveries. But there are people who see to it that green cartons only are allowed in. Suddenly the huge building was lit up, outside by floodlights, inside by the smaller floodlights that had been installed everywhere.

5

Police Commissioner Peiler, wearing riding breeches, hurried through the three floors of the building. His concern: possible hiding-places (among the decorations, in the washrooms) in case of a police raid.

6

When the carnival premises had been sufficiently cordoned off, the General Manager and his staff withdrew to the premises reserved for the organizers. Rehearsal: 120 floodlights. Difficulties arose outside the building in connection with the increasing number of vehicles now arriving.

Interview with an executive of the Patrol and Security Service

If we wanted to, we could make it awkward for fifty per cent of those who insult our guards. Despite all precautions, some gatecrashers manage to slip through every year and join in the carnival. These ineligible persons usually are the ones who insult our staff.

They frequently enter by way of the heating conduits, or they jump onto the roof from adjoining buildings, or they cause a commotion at the entrance and slip in during the general confusion. Whenever there is a ruckus at one of the entrances we assume, and rightly so, that some gatecrashers are creating a disturbance under cover of which they sneak in. Our staff always carry arms. However, they have instructions to resort to their weapons in exceptional circumstances only. We cannot permit the necessary task of providing security to take human lives. After all, not only would we be endangering the lives of those people, although we would shoot at their feet: we would also jeopardize the safety of our officers who risk transgressing the bounds of self-defense. For cases of disturbances of the peace reported by us, the courts pass maximum sentences of three months, with or without probation; for all cases of bodily injury and threats: according to actual or potential damages. Illegal ingress through entrances not known to us is punished by the courts with detention only. We therefore usually refrain from reporting such cases and only go after those who insult our officers. The courts as well as the carnival authorities do not take our work seriously enough because they are not familiar with the difficulties involved. It is our aim, however, to perfect the capacity for compromise and firmness of our patrol and security system and to provide proper protection despite understaffing. We have to adapt our security methods to a changing world, but at the same time we need the co-operation of the public. Many people still feel that those who slip through the Patrol & Security system possibly contribute to a not inconsiderable degree to the general gaiety and are perhaps more suitable types for the carnival than those who have lawfully produced their entrance tickets. Nevertheless we are obliged to insist on tickets being produced. If only in order to avoid overcrowding of the carnival.

Interview with the leading food chemist of the Food & Drug Bureau in the Ministry of Trade & Commerce

Some people seem to imagine that they can supply these organizations with all the goods they can't get rid of in the normal way of business. But these gentlemen are profoundly mistaken. As a rule, we report up to forty per cent in affairs of this size, based on some twenty to thirty caterers. The caterers aren't always to blame, either, for they have to rely on the merchandise supplied to them.

The public will buy anything, of course. They think that when it's a carnival they don't have to be careful, that it's a kind of holiday. I must therefore depend to a great extent on my men in the Food & Drug Bureau, who only too often meet with hostility in their work. No one likes to have his appetite ruined, and people love parties. The caterers, on the other hand, say: What are you doing with those wieners, and so on: many caterers refuse to go on selling to my men once they realize they are government inspectors. In such cases the only thing they can do is seize a sample, and if the sample fails to result in a complaint, then they're really in trouble, for then the seizure was unwarranted. But even though the work of our modest bureau meets with every possible hindrance, so far it has never been quite defeated.

The main problem is that the dealers believe they can supply such functions with poor-quality merchandise. I'd hate to tell you what's in those wieners, or what the confiscated wine you see stacked up over there consists of. People become thoroughly unscrupulous the moment they have reason to believe they are no longer dealing with a critical public but with people who are out to have fun. I don't wish to imply that our bureau ought to be any bigger. This is a problem which cannot be solved by imposing controls: it must be tackled in an atmosphere of freedom. However, I would like to contradict our Honorable Minister when he states that all that is necessary is to be aware of the problem. Mere thinking about it has, as far as I know, never yet made a wiener fit to eat again, if I may be allowed this metaphor. But what does matter is wholesome food in a free atmosphere. In the Food & Drug Bureau we perform something of the familiar work of the detective, and it might be a good idea to write a mystery story one day and, instead of setting it among criminals and detectives, write about the Food & Drug Bureau's work in the catering business.

Interview with a representative of the Treasury Department

We walk through the gathering with watchful eyes. Many people think they are not being observed, but they are. No one wishes to spy on them, it is their private life: nevertheless, we see what's going on. If I am not mistaken, it was Ernest Hemingway who emphasized how many facts a writer has to know if he wishes to write only one sentence (which may have nothing to do with what he knows).

We of the Treasury Department are in a similar position. For us life consists of learning, learning, learning. What a lot a tax official must know before he can make a proper decision! I do not wish to enlarge on these difficulties in our search for facts, but I would like to take the opportunity of pointing out that we know how many people take part in the festivities and how much merchandise is consumed. We are aware of the organizers' little tricks, that they have more tickets printed than are sold. We also see through the one about merchandise consumed—i.e., that almost as much goes back to the dealers as was supplied, even though it was sold. Our method is not to compare the quantities delivered with those left over in order to check on the turnover: the trick is based on an inadequate knowledge of our procedure. We are prepared to overlook small discrepancies, but as soon as we find anything involving excise tax we pounce. There have been cases at affairs of this kind where contraband cigarettes and perfume have suddenly turned up and been sold!

Interview with a representative of the police

Carnival? To us it is just a taxable form of entertainment in which the ticket-buying public may participate. You all know that these affairs continually present new problems for the police which have to be dealt with by the same number of personnel. We have an eighteenth-century police force, nineteenth-century forms of entertainment, and a twentieth-century public. Conflicts are bound to arise. Yet the police have shown over and over again that they know how to celebrate when celebration is called for. I need only recall the festivities in Poland and Russia during the war, at Wilkowischen, Vilna, Mariampol, Tauroggen, Kiev, Melitopol, and in the Crimea during 1941 and '42, the Sports Carnival at Kattowitz, the ones at Lemberg and Litzmannstadt in '43, the carnivals in Smolensk, and last but not least the one in Warsaw in 1944. The stiff, old-fashioned type of policeman has given way to a progressive, forward-looking, I might almost say jolly type of police official whose helpfulness the public appreciates more and more. If I may put it this way: nowadays he is regarded virtually as a participant like everyone else, not as the guardian of law and order but rather as part of the organization as a whole. This new image of the police official needs to be carefully nurtured, and the task of the officers supervising the carnival should be interpreted in the same way.

Title of the carnival

The carnival was called "Nights of Agamemnon," because the original plan called for a carnival in ancient Greek costumes (these are easy to make and would have permitted a certain degree of nudity). The costume rules were subsequently relaxed, but the name with its effective appeal was retained. The entertainment programs were called "Waltzes of Love" and "Waves of the Danube." The carnival planners had stage-fright. Would the carnival get off the ground? Would the offensive be successful?

Resistance to the carnival

Efforts to get the carnival rolling were not successful. The well-behaved crowds circulated among the giant decorations, thronging the wide staircases. The crowds pushing their way up and down the staircases in two great opposing streams had been waiting expectantly for an hour. Häbel, Schleicher, Horn I, Horn II, Putermann, and Beier-Müncheberg hurried along the moving column. They kept to the center seam joining the two streams, i.e., the only places where they could make headway. A brief ripple of excitement when some stacks of beer cases collapse somewhere upstairs; animated motion. An exchange of words, but this is not enough to create a different climate.

Should the carnival committee have more stacks of beer cases collapse, so as to relax the atmosphere?

1st floor (Lower Beer Hall)

If only everyone were permitted to undress, oh to take off these Greek sheets, loosen ties and collars, or at least shout Nazi songs (which is prohibited)! Instead: dutifully empty the huge beer glasses.

2nd floor (Ballrooms, Bar, Wine Only)

Gitta and her friends at the table: she took off her jacket and placed her large hands on the sugar bowl, looked down her arms to see if everything was as it should be, whether her hands were placed as they should be: most of all—yes, a horse. I see them like a horse. I see something on wheels, a frame with two wheels underneath. Two little pointed feet, the legs moving like this (she demonstrates how they move), and there's the heel. Gitta's remarks trailed off. No one expected a miracle from this carnival. The crowds milled about, like Christmas shoppers, through the rooms where wine only was permitted.

3rd floor (Upper Beer Hall)

Here there were groups who took offense if people tried to keep to themselves. A girl swallowed some beer from a glass, leaving white foam on her upper lip. She ran her tongue over her lips to wipe them clean; thereupon she was jeered at by people at the next table. At the counter F. let a home economist embrace him, there was such a draft that this was the only way to survive the evening without catching cold. When P. knocked at the door of a toilet, his girl came out with an escort. What is one to do with a girl who says: I feel like eating ice cream till they gas me?

Tending the carnival, I

At last the fanfare, scheduled for 8:30, announcing the program "Waltzes of Love." Instructions to start ahead of time came from the management. Brintzinger and Karlota conveyed the instructions. In fact the program began at once in all the halls but it failed to catch on because the crowds kept circulating. All the program achieved was to provide a new objective for the old movement: the public look at everything that's going on and continue to push forward with deaf eyes; it is irritating to have on the one hand to look where one is going, and on the other to take in the entertainment. Many people have turned up in costume. Others in street clothes, others in evening dress. A kind of paralysis hangs over the people. What are they to do with themselves? Legs move, arms hang down or are crooked in other arms, eyes are overloaded, ears hear the orchestras which are out of reach, hair is untidy. The crowds have brought nothing with them in the first place, so what are they supposed to do with themselves?

Brintzinger, Beier-Müncheberg, Horn I, and Horn II, always at the seam joining the two streams, push their way through to Entrance No. 4, a disturbance is reported there. The men from the Patrol & Security Service have already broken up the disturbance. But even this fracas fails to enliven the atmosphere. The management hits on the idea of removing the light fuses for one minute, simultaneously announcing over the loudspeaker: Eclipse for Lovers. This relaxes the tense atmosphere.

While the lights are out, an instant of panic, then better contact, which persists when the lights go on again.

The bar waitress

She has come down to the beer hall only for a minute. Her pouch: soft leather hanging down from her waist. She pays from her pouch, in which, before paying, her fingers turn over the coins. She has a slice of meat loaf, and when she has finished eating she throws her serviette over the gravy left on her plate. Right after that she leaves. The glass with a tail-end of Cola stands for quite a long time on the table like a miniature grave.

Tending the carnival, II

Horn I, Horn II, Häbel, Schleicher, Pichota, and Putermann, under the command of Brintzinger, Karlota, and Beier-Müncheberg, mingle in pairs with the public and get it into the mood. Karlota and his two men bring a dance band down from the stage, with them they form a line and wind their way like a kind of polonaise around the second floor, followed by the people. It is vital for the management to take ruthless advantage of any opportunity to improve the atmosphere: Beier-Müncheberg's commandos throw a young man out of the ballroom. That welds the people together. The public are gradually directed toward the focal points of the carnival (the beer hall downstairs, and the restaurant tables, wine only, upstairs). To everyone's surprise buses arrive bringing people from the Rhine-Main and Isar-Main areas; people already wearing funny hats and who on their way here, with the aid of some kind of cheap wine, have reached the stage of being able to pump new life into this carnival. There is a hitch at the entrance. The Security Service men try at first to exercise proper supervision; it is not long before their cordon is broken, people pour in and start singing and swaying. They storm the great staircases and those trying to come down are driven along in front of them to the beer hall on the third floor. Naturally a great many gatecrashers have also managed to gain entrance in this way. But how are they to be tracked down? A few corners are roped off, and in these corners a strict inspection takes place. One or two persons are discovered who are unable to produce tickets.

Manfred Schmidt as carnival prince

Earlier in the evening a delegation from the carnival committee had brought him the keys to the carnival building. He had been presented with the keys to the city several days before. Schmidt, still half-dressed, received the little delegation which handed him the keys to the carnival building. They could have given him a better princess for the evening. He said so, and told them to pass it on to the carnival committee.

The princess

Seven taxis were scarcely enough to accommodate the royal party. Many of the vehicles were overloaded—the committee economized where it shouldn't—slowing the column down to a crawl. M.S. had a car to himself. He had some more champagne. The princess got in beside him. She was not ugly, but she was wooden: Schmidt thought it would be difficult to make the public believe in this princess. He tried to start up a conversation with her and gave her some champagne. But he could not get anywhere with her in the car, and she trembled when he put his arm around her, which was not altogether avoidable in the car.

Dispute with the carnival committee

Schmidt wasted precious time in a dispute with the carnival committee, who requested an interview with him as soon as he arrived on the premises. The committee was annoyed that Schmidt had publicly called them stingy. Schmidt found the discussion tiresome. He apologized, but this took time too, the committee being dissatisfied with the first draft of the apology. This led to a delay in the prince's entrance.

Stand by! 120 floodlights!

Midnight

Shouting from entrances Nos. 7 and 11, fanfares, new floodlights outside, all of a sudden lights out—everyone cheering at the momentary darkness, the orchestras descend from the stage carrying lighted candles, they march into the great ballroom at the top of the staircases. Five orchestras in there, each one playing a different piece, enough to leave you gasping: shouted orders, the General Manager appears.

Manfred Schmidt as carnival prince

It was past midnight by the time the procession of carnival prince, Manfred Schmidt, heralded by orchestras, mounted the staircase. The drum majorettes cleared a path, as best they could, for the actual triumphal procession of the prince. The prince, princess, and retinue first paraded through the whole building. The first tableau was planned for the stage in the great ballroom (restaurant with wine only), which the musicians had vacated. For one moment an observer might have thought—but of course this crowd had no observers—that one section of the column threading its way downstairs at the outer edge of the human wave pushing its way up would be so crushed against the railing that the railing would have to give way. In the event of disaster, the people would presumably have clung to one another and large sections of the human chain would have crashed to its death on the marble steps of the lower staircase. Had this happened, the carnival committee would have been found wanting. The row of eleven drum majorettes marched across the stage and formed a square in front of Manfred Schmidt and his court. The leading majorette drew her sword and strode right across the stage holding the sword in front of her right thigh. She was then followed by the other majorettes. Before the ten girls reached the edge of the stage the column divided, now they marched in two parallel lines back to their point of departure. The leading majorette stood in the center of the stage and saluted. This performance took place in the ballrooms (wine only), in the beer halls on the third floor, and then on the first floor.

Death of the bar waitress

Due to the delay, the timing of the prince's entrance clashed with two raids which Police Commissioner Peiler organized shortly after midnight on the second and third floors. He did not expect to find anything. It was merely part of his method to walk through the principal rooms at least once with uniformed officers. Sometimes a person panics and gives himself away. Peiler walked across the bar, toward the counter, accompanied by the officers. When the waitress saw the police, she lost her nerve. It was later established that at that moment she swallowed poison; to the police officers it looked as if she were hastily emptying a liqueur glass.

Peiler realized at once that something was wrong with the waitress. They managed to remove her to hospital without attracting attention, but on arrival life was extinct, so that no further steps were taken. A soft leather pouch was found in the bar. She had no permanent address; the reason for her sudden action could not be established. The festive spirit had naturally gone out of the onlookers, despite the fact that the lifeless body had immediately been covered up and removed.

What was Manfred Schmidt's reaction?

News of the waitress's death reached Manfred Schmidt just as he was preparing to enter the great ballroom on the second floor at the head of his procession. After being informed of the death he felt that any further processions would be out of place. The prince and his retinue later withdrew to the rooms in the cellar and were supplied with food and drink. M.S. had to decide whether to try his luck with one of the attractive ladies-in-waiting or call up his wife Helena. He was too tired to start anything. He invested the remnant of his charm in the carnival princess, a Frau M., who was considered influential and might be of use to him one day. What good were the little teenage witches to him when he was that tired?

Outcome of the carnival

After mature reflection—and in spite of his dispute with the carnival committee—Manfred Schmidt came to the conclusion that, all things considered, the carnival had been a success. Not a complete success, but no worse than no carnival at all. The committee was also satisfied with the outcome of the carnival.

II THE PERSON

In contrast to the nineteenth century, we are today in a position to predict to some extent the future development of industrial society. We are faced with the phenomenon that changing industrial society will probably demand the same qualities from all classes of society, and I would list these qualities as follows: first, reliability; *second,* mobility; *third,* a grasp of world issues. *These three demands require explanation.*

Hellmut Becker

Not to thrust one's hand into the jaws of fate, but, as soon as fate opens its jaws, to look around for a different fate.

Beethoven-Schmidt

Curriculum Vitae

Manfred Schmidt was born prematurely on February 21, 1926, in Thorn, West Prussia, the son of a g.p., Dr. Manfred Schmidt, and his wife Erika, née Scholz. He attended the local German elementary school and later went on to high school. He left to volunteer for the air force in spring 1943. When the entire unit was to be incorporated into the *Waffen-SS* he deserted, together with his friend K., and escaped to Switzerland. They took the route across Lake Constance, where his friend K. knew someone and had a concealed boat.

After his arrest in Switzerland, Manfred Schmidt appealed to a former acquaintance of his mother's for help. Aided by this kind friend, he and K. managed to escape from the internment camp to Zürich. Immediately after the end of the tiresome war, Manfred Schmidt was employed by an oil company and sent to Sydney, Australia. He spent some happy years there until he was transferred back to a resuscitated Europe in 1951.

At the end of 1951 he took over an executive post with the firm of B. & Quamp Ltd.; soon afterward, the oil company in Australia, which he had just left, collapsed. Manfred Schmidt had no more influence on this bankruptcy than on Hitler's seizure of power in 1933 or the outbreak of war in 1939, but he saw it coming and got out in time. While with B. & Quamp Ltd. he was popular both with his inferiors and with the directors. His ability to adapt himself quickly to new situations distinguished him from his rivals. Since February Schmidt has been married to Helena K., the sister of his old friend K.

Memories of a love affair

I met F. in Sidney. In those days I was still young and full of enthusiasm. She had some pull with the company and managed to get me a few days off, and we spent some unforgettable days together. She then flew back to Europe. From Alexandria I received a telegram in which she asked my advice: a fly or something had stung her while swimming, and she asked whether or not she should have her leg amputated, as the doctors advised. She wanted me to make this decision for her. I later found out that she had already been dangerously ill for some hours when she wired, but she was waiting for my reply. Naturally I wired: amputate, fully concur with doctors. I had also asked my own doctor. Years later I met her again. Quite a young woman, six months younger than myself, perhaps. She could still go swimming in spite of her stump.

M. Sch. acquires a tan

He lay in the sun, and when his face had that degree of heat which according to experience turns to brown—a lengthy procedure, very hard on the eyes: red-rimmed, because they could not stand the bright light—pimples developed on various parts of his face which ruined the whole thing. He said to himself: A person is only vulnerable as long as he has an objective. Verdun and Stalingrad are classic examples of how leaders run into difficulty because they have committed themselves to certain definite objectives. For example, you will never conquer a woman when you set out to do so.

Manfred Schmidt meets Gitta, who later becomes his girl friend

In July 1954, in response to a friend's appeal, Manfred Schmidt became involved in an unpleasant blackmail affair. Gitta P., at that time the mistress of one of his friends, received threatening letters from a former landlady. But she could not bring herself to part with the considerable sums of money demanded. Besides, there was no assurance that, once payment had been made, the blackmailer would not make further demands. M.S. solved the dilemma without payment being necessary. (He had the blackmail victim go to the police and file a report of attempted blackmail.) When this settled the matter he was, of course, the hero of the day, and the woman swamped him with her friendship. For Schmidt, however, this led to trouble with his friend. Gitta P. was the type that leads to trouble. Manfred Schmidt was willing to help, but not to be taken advantage of. Within a very short time he became sick of this trouble. Gitta's girl friend P. had driven a friend's car without a driver's license and had had an accident; she managed to get hold of Gitta, who had a driver's license and seated herself in the only slightly damaged vehicle. When interrogated by the police she was forced to admit that, at the time of the accident, she had not been behind the wheel. In this hopeless situation she again sought M.S.'s assistance. But M.S. could not stand these helpless creatures who make a permanent condition of their helplessness. The very proximity of such unfortunate people is noxious. It is best to become involved only with people who are consistently lucky. With women this is not always possible, but to a certain extent instinct tells one that it is impossible to love carriers of misfortune. Needless to say, Manfred Schmidt gave the girl the benefit of his advice. But that was as far as his interest went.

He wins over a waitress

Are you just helping out here, or do you work here permanently? The waitress said: Temporarily. He watched her intelligent movements as she cleared away the debris on the table. Temporarily helping out? No, permanently. But I don't know for how long. He disliked the previous employees—not because they did not bring him what he ordered, but because of the unintelligent movements with which they served it.

Nothing is more important than intelligent service, he said. She would bring him his coffee at the precise moment he placed the last morsel in his mouth. She could not help laughing herself at her timing; soft creases at the sides of her neck when she laughed, but also when she did not laugh.

He left her a handsome tip and continued to do so for the next few weeks, he exchanged remarks with her and tipped her. Thus M.S. gradually won over the waitress.

He fortifies himself

Red wine, liverwurst, and bread produced a layer of cement which completely lined his stomach. This enabled him to keep going.

He observes a waiter

On his buttocks the waiter carries a pouch divided into two compartments. Acutely sensitive to every movement of this pouch. While he is standing around, he fingers the loose change in the pouch. In this restaurant coffee is served by the pot only.

Manfred Schmidt calls on his former girl friend L. in her last hours

One perfect sunny blue day—after breakfast, which he managed to have at seven, although most of the coffee shops do not open till later—Manfred Schmidt thought he would like to call on L. The air was still cool. He went to see L., with whom he had spent some pleasant days in Trident not long before; but now she was quite ill. Still, he hoped she would not make things too difficult for him.

L. opened the door wearing a silk kimono, white with a pattern of cherry blossoms, tied with a sash; she had pulled it around her in bed because she felt cold. A pretty face, much too small, around which her head had grown to normal adult size. Small hands, body, limbs of various age-categories. As soon as he entered she had to answer the phone, and this gave him a chance to have a good look at her again and take her all in.

When she had finished phoning (in bed again now, a traveling alarm clock on the bed next to her pillow, everything else nice and tidy too), he tried to start something with her, but she merely turned away. Probably he had neglected her too long. He got off the edge of the bed and went into the next room to turn on the little radio and stirred the cup of coffee she had left there for him. Soon it occurred to him for the second time that day that he might be able to persuade her after all. But because of her previous refusal this notion evaporated. Before he had finished his coffee—and when he looked across again to the radio—the light had come on behind the panel.

He made himself comfortable in the apartment. When the doctor arrived she asked him to go into another room. When the doctor had gone he wanted to give her a cold shower, an old-fashioned remedy said to be good for stomach-ache, but she didn't want that either. He sat listening to the radio and told her to call if she wanted him. After a time he went over to her again and asked her if she liked him at all, if it made any difference to her whether he stayed or not. He reminded her of the time in Trident. She groaned, lying on her side, the quilt drawn up almost covering her head, or at least the thin, sheet-covered edge, the way one stuffs a handkerchief in one's mouth and bites on it. He tried to massage her stomach, but she merely pushed him away when he went too far. He criticized her for her attitude and her coldness.

As the afternoon wore on her condition became worse. She had cramps, but he was still too offended to pay any attention. He simply did not go near her. It was only when she had been groaning for rather a long time that he phoned the doctor again. He did his best to distract her by trying to get her in the mood. But she was grouchy, and whatever he did hurt her.

It turned out to be difficult to get hold of her doctor. At first, because of the way she had insulted him, Schmidt had not made any serious effort. He tried to cheer up the girl, who was getting steadily worse, and to kiss her; she didn't understand, she didn't know what he wanted, behaved awkwardly when he put his lips on hers. Not until much later did he realize he was in the presence of someone who was actually dying.

He was scared, but then he felt he ought to give her one more thrill before she died. In fact he made preparations, but they bogged down in the clash of emotions. He remade the bed for her and carried her around the room. She whimpered incessantly and remained doubled up while he unfolded and shook out a clean sheet. Then he laid her on the freshly made bed; phoned various doctors, even called a hospital, but none of them wanted to send anybody. She died at the very moment he seemed to be getting somewhere. By being sufficiently insistent on the phone he finally achieved success. Fifteen minutes later the doctor was there.

Manfred Schmidt in an embarrassing situation

M.S. was embarrassed by the large bluish-brown bruise on his neck given him by Aina Sp. His shirt was rather crumpled, and there were probably some red marks on his collar, he had no time to go home that morning. He had to go to the meeting, at which directors would be present, the way he was. In this state he took in nothing of what was being said. The bruise was almost exactly below his jaw and was practically impossible to hide. That day one of the directors asked him for a brief résumé. Schmidt was obliged to ask leave to remain seated during his short address. That evening, due to lack of consideration, Schmidt was saddled with entertaining some company guests from Venezuela. He was afraid they would be able to smell where he had been, especially in view of the greenish-blue bruise, which he inspected at regular intervals in a cloakroom mirror. It is possible to survive even such an evening as this. It was all most unpleasant, sitting around in this shirt and being asked questions. What was he to do? Quit this type of life because it leads to such unpleasant evenings?

Christmas Eve
Manfred Schmidt had sacrificed everything in his life which he did not want, but he still had nothing. He went on the principle that every sacrifice clears the way for something else and is thus indirectly profitable, and that, if one can only get rid of enough things one does not want, one is bound gradually to get close to the things one does want. All that happened, however, was that the sacrifices impoverished him —which did not alter the fact that he had no desire to be without the sacrifices either. In former years it had been his practice to celebrate Christmas Eve with some of the men from the office; now he had given that up too.

He follows the slow dying of the city that is to be observed only on Christmas Eve, since the city's resemblance to a corpse on ordinary Sundays and holidays, when one wakes up and looks out onto the street, is a *fait accompli*. But on Christmas Eve one can watch the streets gradually dying. It would be dangerous to become ill now, for it is impossible to find a doctor. He is looking for a restaurant where he can still get something to eat. He asks some people who direct him to a place they believe is still open. But when he arrives it is closed. Search for shelter alternating with human kindness, neither of which, however, is capable of locating a restaurant for him. When he does find a place open, he asks the waiter, who politely puts an arm around his shoulder (human kindness), whether there is any room. Every seat is taken and he has to wander around several times among the occupied tables (search for shelter). A customer asks him: Are you sure you don't bite? For a moment it looks as if there might be room, if they squeezed up a bit, but his hopes are dashed. Although the waiter sticks by him to the very end and gives him advice, he is obliged to leave this ark in the dead city. The morning papers had already given up printing political news. People are engrossed in their holiday preparations and handle the day with great care so nothing will happen to impair the mood. After a while Schmidt finds a restaurant where he can get some coffee. But here too he has to leave right afterward. Two women emerge from the night club one floor up, with their escorts, who are putting on their coats. The women are still warm: they go over to the juke box and warm themselves as if it were a little stove. Just one more please, they say, when the proprietor tries to prevent them from feeding the machine. They order a taxi and leave the taxi waiting outside until the music is finished.

Schmidt follows the gradual death of the city; he celebrates Christmas Eve by getting an impression of the dead city. He calls up girl friends, though he doesn't expect them to be home. He feels a great longing for them and cannot remember his reasons for leaving them. He calls up A. and is nonplused when he hears her voice over the phone.

She is alone, and he invites her over. He sends a taxi to pick her up. When she actually rings twice and is there at the door: a miracle is born to us this day. Schmidt brings out a bottle of champagne and rests his head on her shoulder. He shows her how much her nearness means to him; he explains at length how much he has changed; yes, he even believes he loves her now. But he does not grasp the situation, and respects her request not to fall on her immediately. He does not want to become involved. She stays over in his apartment, but things are no longer the same. His nervous system has been overtaxed by the excitement of her coming, and although he is no longer scared of the dead holidays after Christmas Eve, since he knows he has company now, he needs to take a breather. He cannot get rid of the tension in his stomach area. He finds it impossible to approach the woman successfully, and talks rather too much about this point. He loses the child—if one may compare his altered emotions since she came to him with a child or a miracle—and his subsequent success comes too late to do any good. It is in a way something like a second miracle, this success, but Schmidt has meanwhile reverted to his pattern. His victory helps to convince him. Everything is as before (the gamble before knowing a city, the gamble before knowing a woman).

She visited him once more between Christmas and New Year. Then life began again. Right after New Year's Eve there was a lot going on. He lost sight of her.

Application

My name is Manfred Schmidt. I am married, no children, and was born February 21, 1926, in Thorn, West Prussia, the legitimate offspring of Dr. Manfred Schmidt, general practitioner, and his wife Erika, née Scholz. I attended the local elementary school and later went on to high school, from which I graduated (war-time matriculation) in the spring of 1942. In the summer of 1945, after a brief period in the army and some time in Switzerland, I accepted a post as engineer with the firm of Pignatelli & Cie. in Sydney, Australia. Immediately after my appointment as vice-manager I gave up this

position, interesting though it was, and applied to the firm of
B. & Quamp Ltd. in Frankfurt-am-Main. I worked for this
company for a number of years in various places. Since I was
anxious not to devote my entire career to one type of business,
I decided in March of last year to join the firm of Helldorf &
Co., lumber wholesalers, a company offering me excellent opportunities to gain experience in the import of teakwoods and
where I was also put in charge of sales. I have no reason to be
dissatisfied with the broad scope of my duties with this firm.
Nevertheless, I am prompted to submit the enclosed application in the belief that it is likely to improve my prospects.

III   SPECIMEN LOVE STORY

(The Time with Gitta)

Gitta as the young mistress of an old farmer

She was embarrassed by her partner's teeth and therefore
kept her mouth closed. She sticks her tongue into a bottle of
Coca-Cola but can't get into the narrow opening and has to
laugh terribly. Her tongue vanishes into her mouth. Her arms,
very pale, with vaccination marks, muscular under the white
skin, bluish where the veins are: like a dog she pokes her head
toward the carnival farmer to tell him something: rather high
voice. With a wide gap between her front teeth, which makes
her mouth seem attractive; she keeps her lips narrow, so no
one can see the gap.

She yawns, her mouth narrow, she wants to tell this man
something but is stopped short by the unpleasant front teeth
he displays and cannot bring herself to laugh again for a long
time. Her golden-brown eyes, with some reflections in them,
looking quietly around, beyond, till once again she pokes her

head forward like a dog and says something in a high voice.

She was ashamed to be seen by Schmidt in the company of this farmer, who was dressed as a pierrot. The man was trying to paw her while he swallowed small mouthfuls of wine. Needless to say Schmidt rescued the girl at once from this impossible situation. He took her home with him. That first night with Gitta was a complete failure. She became impertinent. While making an effort to be nice and gloss over his fiasco she became impertinent.

The trip to the Isle of Sylt

It rained the whole day. Once, quite early in the morning, they ran through the rain down to the beach in their bathing suits. Dull gray sea, luminous white crests on the breakers. They just splashed about a bit at the edge of the water but did not dare go into the sea because of the wind. Oddly enough there was no warning notice for bathers.

The rest of the day they spent in bed reading, each surrounded by books and magazines. Now and again one of them would read something out loud to the other. At other times Manfred Schmidt would have a long sleep while his girl friend Gitta read her novels. He was not interested in reading. Nevertheless he found this rainy day pleasanter than those previous exhausting days of sunshine when one always had the feeling of missing something.

At a party of some importance, to which he takes his attractive girl friend Gitta

Everyone was aware that Schmidt knew something about Emperor Frederick II in Sicily (from some excursion or other he had made to Sicily). In order to impress the directors, who had also come to the party, he brought up this very subject. It was most embarrassing for Gitta. But she didn't want to interrupt him because she could not be sure how he would react.

With his intense blue eyes and the hard black stars in his eyes. He had a handsome head and it probably functioned quite efficiently, but it was put to very limited use. He had some kind of inhibition about using it. She brought him some cigarettes and a glass of the champagne with which the waiters were standing around. She tried to pry him loose from the group in which he was holding forth.

A bone of contention between Gitta and M.S.

I can't stand it when he says:
Let's not jump the gun.
Tomorrow is another day.
How do we know we'll still be here tomorrow?
Let's wait and see what happens.
That's a long way off yet.
There's no telling what will happen between now and then.
Some built-in inhibition prevents him from using his intelligence, unless he is dealing with things he can see. His intelligence is the slave of those eyes.

Memories of a love affair

I hate Sundays because they show how little is left when there's no work to do. On a Sunday during the war I had to fill in for the supervisor at our air force hospital. The doctor in charge and most of the nurses were away. About eleven o'clock a Frenchman was brought in who had been shot by mistake. He was one of the foreign workers. The idea was to try and repair the unintentional damage at the hospital without having to report the case. Our instructions were to keep the workman on a stretcher till the doctor came back. He lay there quite quietly, now and again complaining, but we could never make out what he was saying. He had hollow cheeks and coarse lips, the tips of which protruded like a child's. Occasionally someone would walk by outside on the street. The hospital was housed in what used to be a school. Those empty streets made me feel physically uncomfortable. The Frenchman died bit by bit in the course of the afternoon, but not quite, so that, in the midst of the food and cups of coffee with which we had surrounded him, in case he felt like having something, he went on quietly moaning. He had ugly hair, plastered down with water, which had survived the shooting in a plastered-down condition. He would not let us touch the wound. In the afternoon I phoned E., who had a war-time job in a hotel in this small town, and asked her to come over. We fixed ourselves up in a secluded corner of the elementary school now serving as a hospital; it was the first time we had improvised anything like that (which corresponds after all to the quite natural instincts of childhood and nest-building), and although I didn't count on success that day, as I felt I was too ill-at-ease to satisfy her, she said something very nice about it to me on a later occasion, and when we talk about it we still sometimes mention that Frenchman, whom the doctor visited in the evening.

Reconciliation

A crisis between Manfred Schmidt and Gitta lasted nearly six months, without either of them becoming truly aggressive. Neither of them lost their temper, and it was almost all over when Gitta had a bright idea and they decided to take a trip. She would have had a lot more bright ideas if instead of a single happy afternoon it had been a whole series of them. But the exception was enough to give her the idea of the trip.

An impulsive stopover in the mountains, because they

found the mountains impressive and wanted to make some decisions. So they got out and looked for a hotel. They could not get a room, but one of the big hotels still had a vacant bathroom. They took the bathroom, and the hotel fixed it up for them as best it could.

They ordered the full dinner, there was no choice, but they were compensated for the appreciable financial outlay by coming across an empty English biscuit tin when they were changing in their bathroom and, pleased with their find, they appropriated it. Compared to their situation in the train they felt much better off, and they finally made up while they were waiting for the second course.

Later on they experimented to see if they fitted into the bathtub, which took up most of the space. But it was too narrow in there for two, and they chose the operating table which had been brought in for them and set up as a bed. It was a spotlessly clean room, the fresh white bedlinen smelled of detergent, it was very hot, so hot that their ears got red, they cleared away some black garments that lay around. Everything was so clean and tiled and so overheated, only artificial light in this little bathroom, pleasantly full from the large meal, now and again someone would hurry along the corridor outside, it was so hot they couldn't be careful too. They could think of no better way of showing they had made up than this. They could have devoured each other, but they confined themselves to being careless.

Gitta's monologue

Should Gitta become a mother? Should she take steps? Act on her own, or ask Manfred Schmidt? Latest possible time is the end of the third month. During these days of doubt Schmidt sent Gitta three red roses, delivered by a Fleurop messenger.

Manfred Schmidt strays during this period

The girl Carmela Pichota, alias Lastics, was born in 1926. At the age of sixteen months she fell into her mother's laundry tub, was lightly scalded, skin grafts, the child made a good recovery. No further incident until she was seventeen. As an army nurse, age seventeen, a love affair with a considerably older married man who was convalescing. As soon as he left the hospital the affair was over for him. For her this was a shock. Four abortions in one year, she was now eighteen. During the next couple of years she studied home economics.

I ought never to have got involved with her. As a matter of fact, I disliked her. I had not noticed what an unlucky person she is.

His girl friend Gitta is not going to be a mother just yet

This time she came to the restaurant quite changed and said something under her breath to one of the women sitting there. Whispered conversation. Her complexion was different, light-pale-flushed: white, olive. She lit a cigarette.

Can love be aborted too?

He carried his full tank of emotions to her in this unfamiliar city. Gitta had been waiting at the hotel since getting news from him. She had spent the morning shopping. He came these days from tough, smoke-filled morning conferences. The moment he was with her in the hotel he drew a line under the stale, unprofitable mornings and abandoned himself to her. He did this so often, hammering away at the one point at which new emotions were showing, that soon there was nothing left of them.

(When he arrived he was bubbling over with affection, and completely wrapped her up in it. He radiated almost the whole afternoon. Still fresh from the frustrating activities of the morning. Her mind was a freshly raked garden, and not only her mind, arms too, legs willing and surrendering to him. Lips, warm and soft. Then he stopped radiating.)

Separation

Schmidt and Gitta withdrew for a week to Krefeld, where they didn't know a soul, in order to give birth to their separation in peace. Gitta attended to that for both of them. She was exhausted when the outcome of the seclusion on which she had pinned her hopes was separation. Schmidt financed a trip for her to the North Sea and went with her for a few days: he let Gitta sunbathe in Rantum. He was satisfied with this solution and only half-believed in the separation, as he was with Gitta every day, he enjoyed freedom in theory and attachment in practice. He looked forward to a winter with Gitta, for he assumed that their relationship would now blossom again. Greatly to his surprise, however, once he had left Rantum the separation turned out to be a *fait accompli*. You become entangled with guilt. But what else can you do?

He is suddenly reminded of Gitta

A streak of hair below the kneecap growing from right to left. Otherwise there was no resemblance. The woman was sitting with her legs crossed and wondered, although she did not raise her eyes from her newspaper, why the man—they were the only passengers in that compartment—was looking so fixedly at her knees.

Portrait of a happy girl with a cold (G.)

She was chilled to the marrow, so she talked more than usual. Aspirin was no use at all. She had borrowed a man's pullover, which had to be brought specially from the cloakroom, and was wearing a fur jacket on top of that, but she was still cold. In front of her stood several hot toddies which the men at her table had ordered for her. Each of them wanted to buy her a drink, and the orders came before the men could agree on only one ordering or a few taking turns. She sat there bundled up as if in the depths of winter.